Emma Watts Phillips

Watts Phillips

Artist and playwright

Emma Watts Phillips

Watts Phillips
Artist and playwright

ISBN/EAN: 9783337386443

Printed in Europe, USA, Canada, Australia, Japan

Cover: Foto ©Raphael Reischuk / pixelio.de

More available books at **www.hansebooks.com**

WATTS PHILLIPS:

ARTIST AND PLAYWRIGHT.

BY

E. WATTS PHILLIPS.

WITH PORTRAIT, AND NUMEROUS FAC-SIMILES OF
SKETCHES AND ILLUSTRATED LETTERS.

CASSELL & COMPANY, LIMITED:
LONDON, PARIS & MELBOURNE.
1891.

Dedicated

· TO

SIR FREDERICK MILBANK.

PREFACE.

WHEN the idea was first suggested of a Life of the late Watts Phillips, or rather a narrative of his career as artist, novelist, and dramatist, the notion was regarded with much doubt. Though he held rank among the successful dramatists of his day, his plays had been for so long unacted in London, that it was feared the public might take but little interest in the book.

The splendid revival, however, of "The Dead Heart" by Mr. Henry Irving, proved that Watts Phillips's name was not lost in oblivion—a fact that was pleasantly corroborated by the circumstance that many of those who were present on the first night of its production at the Lyceum had also witnessed the drama's "first night" at the Adelphi under the management of Mr. Benjamin Webster. Therefore, the Life was at once taken in hand, with a resolution to overcome all probable difficulties, the number and amount of which, in the case of collecting materials, were by no means inconsiderable. Nevertheless, the book is at last an accomplished fact.

I gladly seize this occasion to express my deep indebtedness to Mr. Percy Fitzgerald for the kind assistance and valuable help he has rendered in the arrangement of this record of my brother's artistic and literary life.

My sincere thanks are likewise due to Sir Frederick Milbank and Dr. Ord, who, on learning that letters, drawings, etc., by Watts Phillips, were required, most generously placed the sketches that they had preserved at the writer's disposal, thus supplying, it may safely be affirmed, one of the greatest attractions of the volume.

The sketches which are interspersed throughout the book, with fac-similes of letters attached, will speak for themselves; for the most part they have been placed irrespectively of the text.

The producing of fac-similes of the letters that accompanied the sketches has been considered unique. Not only are they likely to add to the interest of the volume, but also to assist in giving some insight into the artist's temperament.

A high sense of humour and deep pathos were equally blended in Mr. Watts Phillips—the comedy and tragedy embodied in his dramatic works—the laughter created by a "William Kite," "Mr. Aspen Quiver," or "Bottles"—and the higher order of feelings appealed to in a "Robert Landry," or "Job Armroyd."

Of the serious vein, such as that displayed in "The Reaper of the Harvest," there will be found no specimen in this volume; but the humour of the plate, "As it used to was," has been considered worthy of the inimitable humourist Tom Hood.

Attention may also be more particularly directed to the "Noble Tartar," "Swanage," and "My Castle" letters, and to the picture representing the dramatist climbing the greasy pen to procure the family mutton.

More delicately treated, but not less humorous, are the sketches of "A Quiet Family Disturbed," and "The Hare's Toast," the animals in which are scarcely, if at all, inferior to those of the great French animal artist, Granville.

Another plate recalls the period when the artist drew the cartoons for the weekly paper, *Diogenes*, to which further reference will be made. The sketch was prophetic of the result which so speedily followed.

As a delineator of "Cupids," Mr. Phillips might be termed a master; while the plates illustrating "Bird or Heart Catching" and "Health," prove that the graceful delicacy of the idea equalled the graceful and delicate touch of the pencil.

It may not be out of place to mention that several of the sketches—chiefly the humorous ones to his doctor (Dr. Ord) for whom he entertained a sincere affection—were drawn during the silent weary watches of the night, when pain banished sleep.

The present illustrations have been carefully selected as fairly representing Mr. Watts Phillips's artistic talent, but they are only a few of the many with which he so lavishly and generously favoured those whom he held and esteemed as his friends.

Among the possessors of these are Mr. Edmund Yates, Mrs. Stirling and Mrs. Rochfort ("Miss Herbert"). The vestibule of the Madison Square

Theatre, in New York, the writer has been informed, " is hung round with pen-and-ink-sketches " by Mr. Phillips, " beautifully framed," and the fac-simile of two letters to Edward Sothern appeared in the New York magazine, *The Theatre*, date February 7th.

It has also been deemed best, in order not to break the thread of the narrative by an over-crowding of letters bearing chiefly upon one period, to place in an Appendix those others that are characteristic of the writer, and likely to interest the reader.

This book, which has been prepared with much care, anxiety, and—may it be added?—affection, is now launched on the sea of public opinion, and it is earnestly asked of those friends, who yet remember him to whom it refers and with kindly feelings recall his memory, to help ensure it the *bon voyage* which is wished it by

E. W. P.

CONTENTS.

WATTS PHILLIPS:

ARTIST AND PLAYWRIGHT.

CHAPTER I.

EARLY LIFE OF WATTS PHILLIPS—HIS FIRST PLAY.

In the following pages will be found an account of a not very eventful life, which is interesting as the story of a gallant struggle against chequered fortune and the many difficulties which beset the course of the adventurous *littérateur*. The outside world knows little of Watts Phillips beyond the fact that he was the author of some successful plays, such as "The Dead Heart," so recently revived at the Lyceum; but this was only one incident in the troubled career of a really brilliant, energetic man, who had many gifts and accomplishments, with a cheerful, undaunted spirit, which to the last helped him to encounter trials, and a vein of humour which was as much at the service of his friends as it was at that of the public. His story is further interesting as illustrating the unsuspected drudgery which even now, more than ever, attends the course of the hard-working " literary man "— that old tale, in short, as Mr. Forster calls it, " of garret toil and London loneliness," when " the hod" must be carried, and the spade plied, and no "job" can be declined. Old Grub Street and its system still flourishes; and we hear nowadays of the "twenty-five thousand words" exacted for a wage of five pounds and less.

Watts Phillips, however, was inspired by a genuine love of work, and, always versatile and ready, could write novels for the circulating libraries as well as studies of London life for larger and more appreciative audiences; he was poet, artist, dramatist, critic, caricaturist, *comique*, and an admirable, spirited, natural letter writer. It is significant of his cheery character that he expended his happiest and most brilliant conceits in these letters to his friends; whereas humourists of greater note have been careful to economise their wit and put them aside for "copy." These gay effusions, it will be found, are of much interest from their spirit and liveliness, and may be a surprise for many who, after witnessing " The Dead Heart," have come away with the idea that its author was merely one of the ordinary working dramatists. These light, irrepressible, natural efforts have in fact suggested the idea of the story that follows, which is no formal "Life," but an unpretending account of the hopes, fears, and struggles of this bright and buoyant character.

The family was of Irish extraction, his great-grandfather Phillips having come from that country. A great-uncle of the father was a water-colour artist of repute, familiarly known as " Twi-light Phillips," from a work which he had written. The grandfather on the mother's side when a youth had a passion for the stage, and, unknown to his parents, who had a stern, Calvinistic horror of players, obtained an engagement at a local theatre, where in time he filled leading parts. His sister used to let him in at the window on his return. One night his father was induced to go and see a highly promising young actor, and, to his astonishment, in the George Barnwell of the night, recognised his son. He instantly quitted the house and required the youth to give up the stage or be turned out of doors. The latter alternative was accepted, and the young fellow obtained an engagement at Drury Lane. On his way to town he met a young woman in a coach, with whom he fell violently in love, and having offered his hand, it was insisted as the condition of acceptance that he should give up the stage. It must have been unwelcome to learn that what was refused to parental authority was readily yielded to love.

Watts Phillips's father was in commerce in comfortable circumstances, and had married a lady named Watts. • Their son, the subject of this memoir, was born in November, 1825. When a child he showed a strong taste for books and study, as well as for sketching. He did not, however, care to apply himself to the regular course of his school; but, when his parents expressed their wish that he should try and distinguish himself, he quietly replied "that if they wished him to win the prize he would do so," and without much effort succeeded in gratifying their wishes. All kinds of miscellaneous literature he "devoured," and he had a habit of adorning the margins of his books with sketches and caricatures, admittedly of promise.

Being now a young fellow established in London, his inherited taste for the stage began to show itself. He read and re-read the old dra-

Eagle Lodge
Edenbridge
Kent dear
21st

My dear Mr. Wilbank—

Nothing could have given me greater pleasure than to have seen you this week but the above sketch represents my present position, writing night and day against time to get over a quantity of Press work by 'Xmas. If you will kindly drop me a line mentioning any time next week that will be convenient to yourself I will make that time my own.

Thanking you warmly for the kind interest you take

I am Sincerely Yours

Watts Phillips

matists, Ben Jonson, Marlowe, and others; was introduced to the theatres, and to "the world behind the scenes." He became acquainted with the leading actors, and determined himself to become an actor. Mr. Serle, who died recently, and was then acting manager under Macready at Drury Lane, undertook to instruct him in elocution, and assured him of success. He was on friendly terms with the once attractive Mrs. Nesbitt, who encouraged him in his professional hopes. Indeed he seems to have possessed the invaluable gift of attracting friends and acquaintances, for we find him, almost at starting, though a youth, firmly established in the leading theatrical *coteries.* He was found to be an entertaining, pleasant young fellow, full of "cleverness." With the genial and grotesque Buckstone he was a special favourite.*

He was already cultivating his literary taste, and was particularly interested in artistic criticism.

---

* He could venture on such liberties as the following. In the "Kiss in the Dark," the actor, on a sort of raised platform, was exclaiming "Listen to my tale of woe," when his friend, who had concealed himself behind, kept "prodding" the actor's leg with a pin, to his annoyance. Angry expostulations, "Be quiet, you fool!" were mingled with "O listen to my tale of woe." It is curious now to imagine such want of discipline behind the scenes. The same kind of incident is related of Elliston.

He was also studying painting, practised the art of etching, and acquired a facility in humorous sketching and airy caricature. Such facility did he find in this last department that he began to have doubts as to the wisdom of the choice of profession that he had made. When the time for his *début* drew near, which was to be at Edinburgh —he had already purchased his wardrobe—his father urged serious objections, and in consequence he hesitated, taking the pros and cons once again into serious consideration. The father then offered, if he would abandon his purpose, to apprentice him regularly to the popular master of caricature, George Cruikshank, with a view of learning the art and craft of illustration of books. As the real inclination of the young man lay in this direction, he no longer resisted, and abandoning the stage, entered with ardour on the study of his new profession.

Cruikshank, an old friend of the family's, was glad to be of service to them in this way. His dramatic illustrations to " Oliver Twist " were then (1837) attracting equal admiration and astonishment. He had found a pupil of extraordinary promise, who, had he devoted himself seriously and without distraction to study, would certainly have made a reputation. At this time caricature enjoyed an extraordinary favour. The public was not then accustomed to a regular weekly budget of fun and humorous sketches, but each absurdity as it occurred suggested a hasty but spiritedly drawn satirical etching, duly coloured, which drew crowds to the shop windows. A sort of pictorial story was equally relished, a small tract, or series of grotesque incidents, with a line or two of ludicrous description under each plate. There were scarcely half-a-dozen professors of this style—the Cruikshank Brothers; Robert Seymour, inexhaustible in his sketches of Cockney sportsmen; " H. B.," or Doyle, who confined himself to politics; Heath, and one or two more.

Another "shop window" artist of much spirit and versatility was Alken, a dozen of whose sketches, brilliantly coloured, were issued on a sheet. The drawing was admirable, correct, and finished. The text appeared above, below, and in all sorts of corners. The Cruikshanks followed the ancient precedent left by the Gilrays and Rowlandson, of making the sentence issue from the mouth of the figure.

At this time Phelps, one of the conscientious reformers of our stage, was educating the honest

B

natives of Islington to the appreciation of sound acting, and good old pieces. It is pleasant to think of his phenomenal success, and the performances at Sadler's Wells will always have a place in the records of the stage. The young man was attracted to Phelps; the grim tragedian made him his friend, consulted him on his plays, and adopted his suggestions in their production. They further joined in preparing various pieces of the old dramatists, such as "The Fatal Dowry," "Rule a Wife and have a Wife," and the rather untractable "City Madam." These were the palmy days of Sadler's Wells (1844), and the experiment excited much sympathy and interest, though it scarcely turned out profitable. The young man, be it recollected, then not twenty, was also adopted into some lively coteries that included Mark Lemon, the Broughs, Mayhews, Albert Smith, and Douglas Jerrold; and, to secure or maintain his reception, he must have been able to produce his patent of wit and vivacity.

He was now so encouraged by his progress under Cruikshank's teaching that he formed a plan of going over to Paris, and of learning what he could from the French caricaturists, then admittedly the first in this line of art. It may be suspected,

" Oh!" "he" has fallen
Into a pit of Ink that the wide Sea
Hath drops too few to wash him clean again"

Much Ado About Nothing
Act 4th Scene 1st

however, that his mercurial nature was attracted
by the sketches of student life in the Quartier
Latin drawn by his friend Albert Smith in the
" Adventures of Mr. Ledbury." This visit to Paris
introduces us to the pleasant series of letters written
with affection and vivacity to his family, and which
minutely records his life and adventures.

The incidents of his journey to Paris he de-
scribes at great length, but with a pleasant enthusiasm :—

" How shall I excuse myself to our mother, yourself,
and all the others, for not having written a few lines before
this? Truth is the best apology and the one I am most
accustomed to, therefore I own that from the time I first
landed at Havre to my arrival in Paris, I have been so
engaged wandering about from one place to another as
scarcely to find time to eat, much less fill a sheet of paper
with disjointed scribblings, too often only interesting to
the party who indites them.

" As regards my sea voyage I have but little to relate,
excepting that the passage was a rough one, and I was too
late on board to secure a berth; consequently passed the
night on deck. This I cared not a jot for, my internal
department—to my unspeakable pleasure and astonishment—remaining perfectly quiescent, and I found the man
at the wheel—an old seaman—a most eccentric individual
—a sea Epicurus, who considered the ' art of enjoyment
was the end and aim of existence.' ' My children shall
never desire my death for the money they be like to get

B 2

said he; 'for if at the week's *end* I should find enough in
my pocket to buy a quid of 'bacca, why I'm a traitor to my
principles. That's my philosophy.' To a remark of mine
he responded, 'It's all very well, you know, for the clergy
to talk of a *hereafter* and revelations, arn't it their trade?'

"I girded up trunks and departed for Rouen *par
diligence*. The journey was a most pleasant one. Seated
in a *coupé* I chatted with the conductor, a capital fellow,
who, understanding a little English (Heaven knows where
he picked it up!), rattled away at a fine rate. He certainly
was most amusing, nodding and winking right and left at
every female face that chanced to catch his eye, as we
clattered through the villages, evidently, by his own
account, on intimate terms with one and all of them. He
lied through thick and thin in an off-hand style Mun-
chausen himself might have envied. There was not an
inch of road but he knew its history, or something relating
to it. Indeed, he gave me a brief digest of the history of
Normandy, which certainly possessed one merit, that of
novelty, for he informed me that the Normans conquered
England about three hundred years ago, and moreover
prophesied, 'without meaning offence to Monsieur, oh, no!'
that the like feat would be repeated, ere long, solving all
my scepticism with an ease and nonchalance that led you to
believe that politics were not so difficult a business after
all; at least in his hands they ceased to be prosy—a talent
which many a statesman might cultivate with profit. He
was so agreeable a companion that I parted from him with
regret. There is nothing that gives a cigar such gusto as a
fine country road and a droll coachman to chat to. I
wished at the time that my governor had been seated
beside me.

"The country all the way was beautiful; but Upper Normandy and Southern England are as like each other as two dominoes. Had it not been for the houses that dotted the landscape, and the remembrance of a fifteen and a half hours' voyage, I could have fancied myself still at the other side of the Channel, but the houses, that look so red and white against the green fields or shadowy foliage, their gilded vanes glittering in the sun, when once seen cannot easily be forgotten. There is scarcely any difference in their architecture for miles after leaving Havre. They are, one and all, Noah's Arks—yes, the Noah's Ark of our childhood."

Having settled himself in the capital he lost no time in securing a master. He presented himself to Aubert, the publisher of Gavarni's works, and showed him his sketches. The publisher encouraged him, saying that he could make five or six pounds a week in Paris. He hired a studio, sharing it with two other artists, and set to work.

In 1846 we find him pursuing his studies, full of enthusiasm, and, being a pleasant, vivacious young fellow, soon made friends on the boulevards, and in the Quartier Latin. This sort of companionship was not improving for a youth thus cast unprotected upon the great world of Paris. With Gavarni the caricaturist he was much delighted, and his free and happy method of sketching was founded chiefly on that of Gavarni's.

At this time the French caricaturists and artists exhibited a wonderful freedom and mastery in the use of lithography. This brilliant and delightful art has, in England, fallen more and more out of fashion, until it has almost disappeared. No one can have an idea of what fine lithographic work is capable until they have seen the ordinary illustrations of works of "luxury" issued in the days of Louis Philippe. What is so surprising are the rich effects, the depth of tone, the elaborate and delicate workmanship. It was in immense favour as a medium for portraits, and for those innumerable "galleries" of political persons and others which were then in fashion. To this day, it would seem that the *Charivari* adopts the same medium, which allows the artist the dash and freedom of the crayon.

After a short visit to England he returned once more to Paris to witness the revolution of 1848, of which he furnished some vivid sketches. He had even a narrow escape of his life. Some of the revolutionists, hearing that there was an Englishman in the house, paid a domiciliary visit, and, when they were refused admittance, dis-

Eagle Lodge
Eden Bridge
Kent. Jany 26th

Dear Mr Milbanke

I should have written before this
in Reply to your kind letter but have been
awfully bored by a thousand things which
required my immediate attention. Had
I known my last letter would have had
the good fortune to pass into Miss Milbanke
it should have contained something
more pleasing than complaints against
the English climate and sketches of
Irish mis-management I would have
powdered it all over with Cupids &
hung them round her pillow with threads
of gossamer

charged their muskets through the panels of the door. But through the kindness of the concierge's wife he had previously contrived to make his escape. On this hint he thought it prudent to set off for Boulogne to wait events. But he took much to heart this interruption to his studies, and anxiously sought his father's advice as to what he should do.

" There are two steamers," he wrote, " commissioned by Government to be in this port so as to be ready to take off the English residents in case of *need*, but Boulogne appears *very* pacific at *present*. If you think I had better remain here for some little time, please let me know at once. When I am sure of the position England means to adopt, and know that Paris is *quiet*, I can return. The reason I ask your advice is that my prospects there seemed so promising, the engravers and publishers so much in want of artists, that I am loth to throw up such a chance, having received some excellent offers, which this unfortunate revolution has hindered my accepting. I do not see, if England rest quiet (which the French fear she will not, but hope she will—the *men* of France, I mean), why I may not return in a month and resume studies."

The result was that he proceeded to Brussels, where he stayed but a short time, and returned to England in 1849. He at once turned his talents to profit, and was engaged by Mr. David Bogue to furnish him with comic sketches, presenting a story

—a form of publication then in fashion. Such was " The History of an Accommodation Bill," " How we commenced Housekeeping," " The Bloomers," and " A Suit in Chancery." These trifles exhibited at least spirit and cleverness. He presently returned to Paris, with the view of placing himself under Paul De la Roche, and, I suppose, " going in " for the grand style.

My very dear Mother,

Imagine how very anxious I have been for news from home. The long silence made me think all kinds of pleasant things, the more so, as Annie's late epistle gave so melancholy an account of father's being attacked by the enemy of the human race—lumbago. By-the-bye, whether from sympathy, leaving off my flannels, or *both*, I know not, but I've had some severe twinges in the joints. They have now left me, for which I thank God! but 'for all that I have received' I am anything *but* thankful. I frequently hope that father's bulletin is equally good, but between you and me, my dear mother, I think Providence might arrange things better by conferring such little favours as rheumatism, tic doloureux, etc., upon the rich and lazy, whose longest walk is from an easy-chair to a sofa, and spare a man (like a friend of ours) who endeavours to make his life an illustration of perpetual motion. Methinks I hear the curses, both loud and deep, with which the governor welcomed his unexpected, and decidedly un- welcome visitor.

Still, I dare not complain, I reckon now or never is

father's time for head work.   No fear of our wanting subjects of conversation *when* we meet; give him rein and
leave him to himself, and I'll always bet a . hundred to one
on the *Favourite*.   That's very respectful for a son to a
father, isn't it ?   Never mind, " *honi soit qui mal y pense*,"
and that will not be *you*, oh, kindest and best of mothers !
That *both of you* may never pluck anything but heartsease
in the " Garden of Life," is the fervent wish of your very—
Hullo, stop ! I'm not going to finish yet, I've ten minutes
to the good, and when we do meet, though but on paper,
I'm loth to say the parting word.

Paris is very agreeable at present, not *too* warm.   I'm
rather dull, being unable to fix myself till I commence
regularly my struggle for fame.   Ah ! with what pride
shall I lay my first painting at your feet, and may I always
find as kind-hearted a critic !

I've lots of acquaintances here (mark the word !—as for
friends, Cowper and I agree upon that point), who are very
civil; but I want to get to work—real, and well directed
work—and before I return to England I trust to be able to
stand alone.

To all at home, I know not what to say, so shall follow
poor Cordelia's example " love, and be silent."   I should
care little where it might be—Australia, . New Zealand,
Paris, or Seven Dials, so that we were always united in
person and in heart, for

> " No matter where our fate may guide us,
> If those we love are still beside us."

With these two homely, but pleasant lines, I leave you.

After spending some time in Brussels pursuing

his studies, the young artist returned to London. His father, after a serious illness, died, and his son soon found himself thrown entirely on his own resources. For a time he tried to "earn a living" by illustrating slight ephemeral works, and was engaged on a newly-launched comic paper, *Diogenes*, intended as a sort of rival to *Punch*, and long since extinct; very many of the cartoons were of his design. This also furnished him with an opportunity for exhibiting his skill in another department, and he discovered that he had a turn for writing lively satirical sketches, which were likely to bring him more profit than the exercise of his pencil.* At the time there were a number of clever young men, the Brothers Brough, the Mayhews, Edmund Yates, and others, who were busy depicting the humours of the town. These were his friends and associates, and he speedily enlarged the circle.

"In the year 1854 or '55," as one of his friends recalls it, Watts Phillips wrote "The Wild Tribes of London." It was a fair history of London slums, dealing with both Ratcliffe Highway and Seven Dials. One Travers dramatised, and

* Such were "Thoughts in Tatters: by the Ragged Philosopher"—a quaint title.

What do you think of affairs now, and the "*baptism* of fire"? *this* is like it

"Come along Louis! Come along! we've *both* of us been baptised enough!!!"

played it, under its original title for the City of
London Theatre, Norton Folgate, then under the
joint management of Messrs. Johnson and Nelson
Lee. · The piece was very successful, and the
author sold the acting right to the proprietors for
£7 10s., and they sold it to " Barney Egan" for the
Queen's Theatre, Manchester, for £20, and made
over to him the right of acting it in Manchester,
Hanley, Chester, and Wolverhampton.

While thus industriously engaged in literary
work, his connection with theatrical *coteries*
naturally attracted him to the stage and the
work of the stage. He had completed several
dramas, one upon a French subject, " Joseph
Chavigny, or Under his Thumb," whose chances
of acceptance by the managers seemed remote
enough. But a fortunate accident of a very
unusual kind favoured him. He had given the
piece to a well-known theatrical copyist, Mr.
Hastings, to be transcribed. This person, depart-
ing from the mechanical tradition of his tribe, read
as he copied, and was so interested in his work that
he showed it to Mr. Webster of the Adelphi, as the
very striking production òf a young writer that
was worth his attention. The manager read it,
and was pleased. We may imagine the surprise

and delight of the young author when, instead of receiving back his drama fairly copied out, he was invited to a personal interview with Mr. Webster, who promised to produce it. The manager, who seems on this occasion to have behaved like one out of a fairy tale, even asked for other works, and before he had experimented with "Joseph Chavigny," actually purchased two more of the young writer's pieces, "The Two Strollers," and "The Dead Heart." Was ever dramatist thus encouraged in his first attempt?

The piece was produced in May, 1857.* It had rather the air of a French adaptation which may have recommended it to Madame Celeste, who was then an attraction at the Adelphi, and was really "manageress." This lady was one of the earliest foreign broken-English-speaking performers whom audiences have since so indulgently tolerated, and

---

* It was thus cast:—

Joseph Chavigny . . .	Mr. Benjamin Webster.
.Count Gerard de Grandmesnil .	Mr. Billington.
M. de Varennes	Mr. Garden.
Regnier	Mr. Paul Bedford.
Madeline	Madame Celeste.
Madame Moulbaron . . .	Miss Eliza Arden.
Madame Varennes	Mrs. Chatterley.

Charles Selby and Miss Laidlaw also had parts.

who has been succeeded by a regular line of such
exotics. Such intrusions seriously injure dramatic
illusion, and would be resented on any foreign
stage. "Joseph Chavigny" was coldly received.
It may be interesting, were it only for contrast with
the present style of criticism, to turn back to the
commonplace and unrefined tone that was in vogue
in *The Times*. "The new drama," it wrote,
" presents one of those rare cases in which the
critic may conscientiously take part with the
author against the public. Generally the public
is distinguished *by the vast capacity of its swallow*,
and its best counsellors would advise it not to gulp
down too much. In this particular case the
Œsophagus is *unusually* and unreasonably contracted,
and the audience of the Adelphi Theatre may fairly
be reproached by the dramatist for testifying little
gratification when he has laboured much, and *displayed a degree* of talent seldom seen in the dramas
of the present day." "The author," it added,
" might rest satisfied that he had produced one of
the best written pieces of the day; nevertheless he
has fallen upon a time when writing is a secondary
consideration." The same judicious critic considered that the dialogue was distinguished by an
epigrammatic form of no common order. *The*

Era, not then a power in the profession, was prophetic :

"We have not," wrote *The Era,* "for many
years witnessed a piece of such legitimate merit, or
enjoyed a dramatic performance with so much relish
and delight, as we experienced at this deservedly
popular little theatre last Monday, on the representation for the first time of ' Joseph Chavigny, or
Under my Thumb,' written by Mr. Watts
Phillips. . . . After the trite and slipshod diction
to which we have of late been so accustomed, and
which authors are in the habit of using in
ephemeral pieces of the day, to link together the
dialogue of their plots, it is perfectly exhilarating
to listen to the terse and nervous energy of the
language put into the mouths of his characters by
the author of ' Joseph Chavigny.' The piece is
written throughout in a close masculine style that
often approaches the epigrammatic, abounding in
sharp repartee and caustic sarcasm, that reminds
us forcibly of Douglas Jerrold's best mannerisms
not as a dramatist, but in those happy expressions
that form the spirit of his last prose works; and
this is about as high praise as we can award. It is
a style admirably suited for the stage, especially
when blended, as in the present instance, with

his greatest pleasure was sliding
down the bannisters of the hotel
when his meals were ready very
much to the surprise of the waiters

and other flunkies, though I'm afraid
it is the father and not the son who has
really _slid down the bannisters_ ×

come down on the _door Mat_.

pathos and interest. On the whole we most cordially welcome this new production as being the first of what, we trust, will prove a long line of dramas in the right direction, and at once energetic and natural." *

---

* In our day, when a French-speaking waiter has been introduced on the stage and applauded to the echo for saying, " *un siphon, m'sieu' ?* " it is amusing to read that Mr. Webster objected to the words " *de trop,*" which he protested would not " be understanded " of the British public. Joseph Chavigny "coming through the glass doors at the back " exclaims, " I'm *de trop.*" " I'm one too many," was the manager's alteration.

CHAPTER II.

IN those days there was no theatre more popular
than the little "Old Adelphi," so long managed by
that sound, effective actor, Ben Webster. The
style of entertainment rarely varied, being usually
an exciting melodrama of a poignant, touching
interest, and French pattern, or, in many instances,
a simple adaptation of French pieces. Such were
the "Dream at Sea," "Marie Ducange," "Janet
Pride," as well as that interesting, romantic, and
well-constructed play, "Victorine, or I'll sleep
upon it"—the pattern of many more—which
enjoyed an immense popularity all over the kingdom. An "Adelphi drama" became a special
type; and, distressing as might be the story, it was
invariably relieved by a strong comic element, displayed to extravagance almost, by the humorous
Wright and his colleague, Paul Bedford—pillars of
the house. There was the grim O. Smith, gifted
with a gruesome face and manner, and invariably
cast for some smuggler or pirate, an exaggeration

of villany. Miss Woolgar, still with us, furnished
piquancy and liveliness, or enacted the suffering
heroine; while the manager himself bore the
general weight upon his shoulders. The exposure
of villany often took place at some festive scene or
dance at night, when the company crowded in, arm-
in-arm, to group round, and witness the dying
agonies of the villain, and hear his revelations.
Hence much jesting at the expense of the awk-
wardly behaved "Adelphi guests,"—like Johnson's leg of mutton, "ill-fed, ill-kept, ill-dressed—
later to be happily ridiculed by Mr. Gilbert—though,
in their favour, it might be urged that the guests of
our well-appointed dramas often represent just as
indifferently, though in more becoming attire, the
manners and bearing of the society of *their* time.

At this period each theatre—such as the Haymarket, Sadler's Wells, and the Adelphi, had its
regular "patrons," who came again and again to
" see Buckstone " or to " see Webster," and enjoy a
hearty laugh with Wright. Under the existing
system there can of course be no regular
" patrons," as every successful play is likely to
" hold the field " for six months, or even a year
The " patrons " of the Lyceum and the Haymarket
and the smaller houses, when, for instance,

c

"Faust," "Our Flat," or the "Private Secretary" may be performing for a couple of years, are virtually the whole kingdom, or rather the great kingdom of London—playgoers coming but once or twice to see the favourite play. But under the old system an Adelphi audience would naturally require frequent changes in their entertainment. As the farce was then of importance, persons who had seen the *pièce de résistance*, were gratified with novelties, in which their favourite Wright could exhibit some novel humours; in short, constant variety and new pieces were necessary to maintain the attraction. This, it may be imagined, had a beneficial effect on the powers of the actors, who became practised in all sorts of devices, owing to their being measured for new characters which, to their own surprise perhaps, discovered in them unexpected and unsuspected gifts. It is idle to lament this happy state of things, and it must be admitted that the present system is the proper one, because it is the result of "the form and pressure" of the time, which only a Mrs. Partington would attempt to resist. But it may be imagined what an opening was here for the industrious, versatile dramatist. The manager was then eager to secure pieces suitable for his theatre, being much in the position of the

French manager in the early days of Dumas, who accepted works from all applicants of known ability. But now, when a single play of merit will supply the wants of a theatre for a whole year, the position is reversed. The author of our time may wistfully look back to the palmy days when Webster held no less than three of young Phillips' dramas in his possession, which he produced as opportunity served. As we have seen, "Joseph Chavigny" had appeared, and the author was now impatiently pressing the production of another piece, in whose merit he had an almost extravagant confidence. This was the stirring and picturesque melodrama of "The Dead Heart," which has recently excited so much interest on its revival by Mr. Irving.

In spite of much pressure the manager seems to have long hesitated before producing it, and put it aside until he had brought out its fellows. The author pleaded for his "Poor Strollers" in an almost vehement strain of confidence in its merits, which later seemed to inspire managers with some of his own enthusiasm.

But the rather moderate success of "The Poor Strollers" did not encourage the manager to undertake another venture from the same pen. The

c 2

subject, too, of "The Dead Heart," with its Revolutionary crowd, Bastille, etc., had been treated
only a few years before in an adaptation by
Boucicault of Dumas' "Chevalier de la Maison
Rouge," and this, as Mr. Coleman has suggested,
was likely to have been the reason for holding the
piece over for some years.

Though fretfully waiting for the chance that
was, as he fancied, to make his fame and fortune,
Watts Phillips never relaxed in his ordinary
literary work, supplying articles to the *Daily News*,
and to country papers; besides writing much
in a venture of Mr. Maxwell's, *Town Talk*, one of
the earliest, capricious attempts at what are called
"Society Papers." To this he furnished a story,
"The Honour of the Family," afterwards dramatised as "Amos Clark." His pencil, too, was
busy. Yet it is curious to find how this gay,
buoyant man seemed to have an attraction for
"grisly" subjects, and he now produced a curious
and ghastly work of imagination, relating to the
Garibaldi episode, which struck his friends from its
morbid power.*

---

* This was a Death's Head, *coiffeed* in a low-crowned hat,
wreathing itself with flowers, and bearing a scythe in a rather
jaunty manner. A pretty landscape stretches away in the back-

Ladies and gentlemen are ? Then I've done chatter? I give you the health of the "Talking colonels" who are keeping all the M.P.s in London!

MOUNTAIN DEW

My dear "Mr Milbank"

It seems a hundred thousand years since I last sent you a sketch, but I have been so awfully busy with so many things, above all with removing from Eden Bridge, and, once again, pitching my tent

Oh ...!!!! "Parliament's prorogued and here! Milbank coming !!!!"

But his thoughts were still fixed on the drama, in which he had concentrated all his powers. Mr. Webster, who had his moods of hesitation, could not be induced to move; he saw innumerable difficulties and dangers, and the disheartened author betook himself to his much loved Paris. · "Oh that weary waiting," he said to his friend Coleman; "I can't think of it now without a shudder. I was sick, sore, sorry, and desperately hard up besides." After he had well nigh renounced all hope, he was of a sudden overjoyed to learn that the manager had at last made up his mind to bring forward the piece. This, as will be shown later, was owing to the appearance of Mr. Dickens' "A Tale of Two Cities," which, to his annoyance, seemed to anticipate some of his situations. But now all was *couleur de rose*, and the mercurial dramatist, full of hope and ardour, was already planning new schemes and offering new plays. He wrote—

August 2, 1859.

(In haste.)

MY DEAR WEBSTER,—I feel your prompt kindness very much, nor will my future recognition of it be the less

ground, and the legend "War" is faintly traced. Mr. MacLean was inclined to purchase this design, but thought it too depressing a subject to have a sale.

because I now confine myself to the sincere "I thank you." I DO thank you, and that most warmly.

I am very pleased at the opinion you express that David Fisher will make a hit in "Latour." But what will you do about Catherine? The part is not only a *most* important one in itself, but, if not well acted, fails to give the *requisite* relief to Landry. I increased *her* power towards the end, and it must be great and *intense* to shake the firm resolution of Robert. An inferior actress would fail to convey this.

I shall be all anxiety till I hear how you have got over this difficulty.

" A manager's life is not a bed of roses," says Colley Cibber. It seems to *me* more akin to the gridiron of St. Lawrence.

> " If you want trouble and have too much pelf,
> First take a theatre, then manage it yourself."

I think Miss Kelly will do Cerisette capitally. I wish some little song could be slipped in somewhere for her; it would give relief. She's got what the French call " tears in her voice," and a little song *always* puts the audience in good humour. I remember the plaintive effect of the song in " Green Bushes; " it went through and through my heart, and refined the whole drama.

Couldn't one be introduced ?

I wish Bedford and Stuart were more of a *size*. Do you think Paul would object, *just to oblige me*, to put himself upon bread and water for a week, or, which is more likely, would Stuart go into training—beefsteaks and porter three times a day, with a dose of cod liver oil every three hours ?

Jesting apart, I think Stuart will do Legrand *very well.*

I hope Toole takes to Toupet. I have only seen him once as the Jack Pudding in " Belphegor," and thought it excellently done. . .

Has Wright left the stage altogether ?

I think the spectacular effects of the drama will tell well in the new theatre, which I seem fated never to visit.

. . . I am rapidly polishing up "The Curse of Gold." As a domestic drama, I think you will highly approve of it. It is LAUGHTER, *passion,* and *tears* all of the *homely* sort. The characters are few, and this is how I hope to see them filled :—

Jan Smet (*a sweep*) . .	B. Webster.
Peterkin (*his son*)	Toole.
Simon (*a shoemaker*) . . .	Selby.
Townspeople, etc.	
Dame Smet	Mrs. Mellon.
Katie (*with song*) . . .	Miss Kelly.
Lacemakers, etc., etc.	

The plot is borrowed from a beautiful and simple Flemish story, the stuff is my own, the character of Jan Smet is *made* for you, and I'm sure Mrs. Mellon hasn't *had* a better part than Dame Smet. However, directly it's done, you shall have it for "judgment."

Anxiously waiting to hear more about the Green Room difficulties,—I am, &c.*

Notwithstanding the promise, this was to prove a season of anxiety to the author. So much

* From Mr. Coleman's " The Truth about ' The Dead Heart.' "

depended on the success of this third drama, which had not only to confirm his previous success but to surpass it. He was naturally nervous respecting the casting of the characters; the two or, it may be said, three strong, leading parts in the piece depended so much upon the actors and actresses who delineated them. "Robert Landry" he knew was safe in Webster's hands; he was also satisfied that David Fisher was to play the "Abbé Latour," though he did not imagine the great success which that excellent actor would achieve in the part; but it was with consternation he learned that Miss Woolgar had been cast for "Catherine Duval." For Miss Woolgar he had the highest regard personally, and a high appreciation of her histrionic talent in the particular line she had adopted; but "Catherine Duval" was quite out of that line. Indeed it was a part such as she had never before attempted, and she herself at first declined it. In the letter to which reference has been already made, he says: "Miss Woolgar is to act 'Catherine Duval'!!!!! She refused it at first because (very truly) she was not a tragic actress; pressed to do it upon pain of dismissal, she consented. I see now that it is announced in the papers that she is ill, and *may be so* for a time—

but Webster *thinks* not. What a chapter of accidents !" Fortunately the actress recovered in time
to take the part, and the result took the author
as well as the Press by surprise. Miss Woolgar's
"Catherine Duval," full of power, feeling, and
dignity, was a great success, which the author and
the Press warmly recognised.*

* The drama was produced on November 10th, 1859, with
the following caste :—

THE DEAD HEART.

(A Drama in a Prologue and Three Acts.)

The Count de St. Valerie . . .	Mr. Billington.
The Abbé Latour	Mr. David Fisher.
Robert Landry	Mr. Benjamin Webster
Jacques Legrand	Mr. Stuart.
Reboul *artists and*	Mr. Paul Bedford.
Michel *students*	Mr. W. H. Eburne.
Jean	Mr. Moreland.
Pierre	Mr. Conran.
Toupet (*perruquier and coiffeur*) . .	Mr. J. L. Toole.
Jocrisse (*owner of the cabaret " Les Trois Ecus ")* . .	Mr. C. J. Smith.
Baptiste Duval	Mr. Page.
Ferbras (*a blacksmith*) . . .	Mr. Aldridge.
Blaireau (*crier*)	Mr. R. Romer.
Martinet (*officer of gendarmes*) . .	Mr. Howard.
Catherine Duval	Miss Woolgar.
Cerisette	Miss Kate Kelly.
Rose	Miss Laidlaw.

Mr. Billington, then a "leading juvenile," impersonated the son, "Arthur de St. Valerie."

The success was great, even far exceeding the expectations of the manager. The play attracted large audiences. The *Times* wrote :—"'The Dead Heart,' a drama of more weight and more pretension to sustained interest than has been witnessed for a long time at any theatre, was produced last night with distinguished success. The meagre outline which we have given of a piece abounding in strong incidents, and wrought up with a rare degree of elaboration, is necessitated by its extreme length, which caused it to terminate at a late hour. As its success will secure for it an enduring vitality, we may take occasion to refer to it at some future time."

The striking phantasmagorial effect at the close, however, found objectors, notably in the *Literary Gazette*, then an important organ of criticism :—

But a grave fault completes the drama. Catherine learns the truth (that Landry has sacrificed himself for her son) when her son is encircled by her arms—learns it by gazing through the window, and seeing Landry mount the scaffold. But this does not satisfy Mr. Watts Phillips; so the solid walls of the Conciergerie are made to slide up and down, and the audience see the guillotine, and the martyr preparing for the knife. This stage business utterly

The Loan of an Umbrella.

The Return of the Umbrella.

destroys the natural effect of the acting. It makes a really
good and touching drama, beautifully played, terminate un-
naturally, and even absurdly.

The Queen and Prince Consort came twice to
see it, when the house was " crammed." " What
an *immense* success," wrote the author to his sister,
" the play has been ! Have you seen the *Dispatch*,
Telegraph, and *Spectator ?* Webster says it is the
best play that has been acted for *many* a long year !
Fred Jones has written me ten *closely-written* pages
of most *admirable, intelligent* criticism on ' The
Dead Heart' and the actors. He concludes by
terming it the ' *greatest* dramatic work of our day.'
It is largely talked about *here* " [that is in Paris].

The author's triumph, and even exultation, at
having at last secured a solid success, found vent,
in very natural fashion, in a letter to this old
schoolfellow. Unluckily, he was unable to take a
share in either the preparation or the success of his
piece—some shape of *force majeure* preventing his
coming to England. But there were troops of
friends to send him abundant details.

DEAR FRED,

A letter from you is always a pleasure to me,
especially when accompanied by a criticism of *much* value.
You have placed the " first night " vividly before my eyes,

and I sincerely thank you for it. I do not flatter when I
say I know of no modern man, literary or otherwise, so
capable of sterling dramatic reviews. Do not put this as
" a wipe off" for the favourable remarks upon my drama.
You have given me too many *hard* rubs for me not to
know you are conscientious.

Webster is in a state of exultation about the success.
I confess to having been nervous, but *Webster's* confidence
in the piece kept *me* up; a firmer or a kinder friend no
author could wish for.   The same night a telegraphic
dispatch arrived from him, worded in a way I shall not
readily forget, to relieve my most natural anxiety.   There
is *one* thing that has vexed me in the criticisms—the
notion that my drama must be from some French play or
novel.   It is from neither.   As Touchstone says of Audrey,
" if a poor thing it is mine own."   I have a knowledge (from
my long residence) of the French *people*, and know the
literature of the revolution *well*.   My only borrowing was
from an incident related in Carlyle's history (concluding
chapter of third volume), in which an old man, the Marquis
de something, answers to the roll-call in place of his son
(who is asleep) and takes *his place in the tumbril.*

I have never read " Monte Cristo," and let anyone
take up the " Maison Rouge," and point out, if they can, its
similarity *in any way*, but by being in the revolution.   It's
too bad !   But, as Webster says, " we can afford to laugh,"
though my next drama shall be laid in England, and then
there will be no doubt about it; or, if in France, I'll make
the characters behave as though born under " Bow Bells "
and speak a broad Lancashire dialect.

Another drama is wanted.   Can you suggest some
period of history suitable for the stage ?   The " Account

Balanced " will be a safe go, its skeleton now only requires flesh, but Webster wants a telling, *great* (if possible) *English* drama, with effects, for he agrees with you about accessories, and will not shrink from cost if I furnish the staple commodity. He has never changed in his opinion of me for a moment, but has ever been so kind and considerate, so encouraging in all things, and so anxious for my future, that I shall ever do my very best for him.

You've no idea what a storm of congratulations I've had from men whose good word is of value. It gives me heart, and I mean to strive day and night to better my success.

The *Times*, *Telegraph*, *Morning Post*, *Globe*, etc., promise second notices. I don't know whether any have appeared—that they *will*, I know.. Will you kindly send them all to me (I mean every *second* notice) ?

I have conveyed to Mrs. Mellon what I consider my obligation to her. As for Toole, we have had many pleasant talks and meetings in the far North, and I knew he would do his best for my interest and his own, especially as he has a character in a piece of mine forthcoming, to which Toupet is but a patch—a certain Bill Kite or Mr. Accommodation Bill, a gentleman who traces his success in life to "six lessons under the immortal Carstairs."

Again, let me thank you, old schoolfellow and crony, for your long and most welcome letter. I read it by the fireside, and realised the picture you painted.

You know I will do my best to improve my success, especially as the "Hip, hurrah!" so long held back, is coming in on all sides ; and all I can offer to you for your most kind and able criticism is the wish—to borrow from dear old Cowper—that when *next* I ride my race "may you be there to see," and write me an account afterwards.

I am, truly yours,

WATTS PHILLIPS.

But in this flush of success his sensitive nature was to be harassed by those vague and unsubstantial charges of plagiarisms which were to be revived thirty years later. As we have seen, a few months before, in the April of the year, Mr. Dickens had issued the first instalment of his picturesque story, "A Tale of Two Cities," which, as all know, is concerned with some exciting passages in the French Revolution. In so vivid a picture the Bastille, and the prisoners of the Bastille, were likely enough to find a place, and by the time the second monthly portion appeared, the dramatist was aghast at recognising one of the leading situations of his piece.

WATTS PHILLIPS TO WEBSTER.

Ramsey, June 2nd.

Of course, *they will make a play* of Dickens' new tale, "The Two Cities," and (if you have read it) you will see how the character of the man ".dug out" of the Bastille will *clash* with the man in "The Dead Heart," written more than *three* years ago. Knowing your peculiar powers, I wrote Robert Landry *exclusively* with a notion how you

The Small-page of the Ledger
or The Substance and the Shadow !!!

"This is our pattern book ! Every sort of stuff. and at every sort of price You'll find us always ready To SERVE our customers ! "

would *act* that character, and foreseeing the reputation that would arise to me. And now, owing to a *delay of years*, Dickens puts into *words* what I had hoped long ago to see you put into *action*. The tone of the resurrection from the Bastille ought to have been *fresh* in my play, not in his story. It's very heartbreaking.

It will be seen that there is here something in the nature of reproach, as who should say " it is *your* delay that is responsible for all this." Heart-breaking it was, indeed ; and it must have been with yet more serious misgivings that he nervously followed the course of the story—dreading some new, disastrous surprise at every page. By some strange coincidence he was to find yet another of his numerous situations anticipated in Sydney Carton's heroic sacrifice at the close. But the number in which this *dénouement* was developed did not appear until after the play had been produced. Nothing is more singular than these coincidences. It has been often said that a subject is often, as it were, " in the air," and that its " germs " work by a sort of contagion. But the more likely explana-tion is that there is a legitimate development of a dramatic subject which is almost certain to be worked out by capable writers in the same way. No doubt it was the feeling that he had been more or less responsible for this unhappy state of things which prompted the manager to make all the amends he could, by at once putting the play into rehearsal.

Here, however, was the most popular story-teller of the day, who had his many thousands of readers : and some of his strongest situations are found in a play produced before the conclusion of the tale. In the newspapers this was freely commented on, to the distress and vain protests of the author and manager. A new charge was now made that it had been "stolen" from the French. Webster wrote to the *Sun* that it was "perfectly original from first to last to my knowledge, not even adapted from a novel, which does not, in my humble opinion, entitle a drama to be styled original. I trust you will do this justice to a young and talented author, who has nothing but fame to live on." This was in January 18th, 1860. Three weeks later Webster had to make this fresh appeal :—

> New Theatre Royal, Adelphi,
> February 8th, 1860.

SIR,

I should have thought that, after twenty-three years' management, during which lengthened period I have never broken faith with the public, the announcement in my bills for nearly one hundred nights that "The Dead Heart" was an original drama would have satisfied the most sceptical. However, the courtesy and respect for long and truthful service was wanting, and I have been compelled, in the absence of the author, to publicly, by letter, vindicate him from the charge of adaptation, or translation, *vide* the *Morning Advertiser*, the *Sun*, etc., some ten days since. It is also well known—and I can immediately prove it— that " The Dead Heart " was written and paid for years before " The Tale of Two Cities," or the periodical in which it appeared, was dreamed of.

I cannot conceive more ungenerous treatment than Mr. Watts Phillips has experienced, and feel that such attacks are most discouraging to original writing, and to managers who wish to promote it.

The author, indeed, went so far as to say that the piece was " seen by Dickens long ago." It seems that when he first sent the piece to Webster, the latter took it down to Brighton, and there read it to two or three friends, one of whom was the novelist. It was further insisted that the closing .scene was nearly the same as a stirring situa- tion in Dumas'· *Chevalier de la Maison Rouge*, pro- duced in Paris some twelve years before. But the self-sacrifice in question seems to have been but a " common form," for, as Mr. Coleman has shown, and the author, indeed, has admitted, a similar inci· dent is described by Carlyle in his " French Revo- lution." There is something like it, also, in Palgrave

D

Simpson's and Merivale's " All for Her."   It is also
found in Lord Lytton's " Zanoni."   And here
in dealing with this perplexing and oft-debated
question of originality, it may be said that a mere
" situation " is common property, though the mode
of dealing with it and of approaching it, offers
infinite novelty and variety. A dozen painters will
portray the same landscape, each with different
result.   One will only see an effect of light,
another a minute exhibition of leaves, twigs, etc.,
a third, like Corot, will be struck by a feeling of
gaiety or melancholy, a fourth will think only the
figures important. A love scene will strike each
author in a different way. *Character*, in short, and
the display of character, in all its innumerable shapes,
is ever novel and Protean.

As Watts Phillips had anticipated, "A Tale of
Two Cities" was, without loss of time, prepared for
the stage by Mr. Tom Taylor, that admirable,
workmanlike dramatist, whose firm, secure touch,
and perfect knowledge of the stage, was always a
guarantee of success. *   Madame Celeste, so lately

* The superiority of his work is shown by contrast with the
too often loose and meandering style of modern efforts, where so
much is thought to depend on " witty dialogue," as it is called, to
the sacrifice of genuine dramatic effect. In this economy of
mere talk Tom Taylor was conspicuous : he only considered the
business of the scene.

Mr. Webster's partner, had now undertaken management for herself at the Lyceum, and on January the 18th, 1860, the new piece was produced. As Mr. Coleman tells us :—" It was an admirable production in all respects, both as to acting and mounting. Certain impersonations in this drama have not been excelled, perhaps not equalled in our time—notably Madame Celeste's boy in the prologue and her Madame Defarge in the play; the pathetic Lucy Manette of Miss Kate Saville; the Doctor Manette of James Vining; the sympathetic Sydney Carton of poor Fred Villiers, and the wonderful wicked Marquis of Walter Lacy. The two plays ' caught on,' and their resemblance to each other having attracted universal attention, society divided itself into two factions—the Celestites and Dickensites, the Websterites and Phillipsites. Then came accusations and recriminations as to coincidences and plagiarisms, and bad blood arose on both sides."

Thirty years later Mr. Irving, in the full tide of his success, was attracted by the romantic motley shades of character offered by the part of Robert Landry, which seemed to be especially suited to his own gifts, and determined to revive the piece with all the resources and adornments it was

D 2

capable of.   He, however, took the course of adapting it to modern tastes, and subjected it, with Mr. Walter Pollock's aid, to a good deal of "toning down" and polishing, so as to remove the old Adelphic *cachet*.   Some critics, however, urged that the piece would have gained in interest had it been submitted in its original state ; and it suffered by the almost wholesale elimination of its humours, which were so racily presented by Toole and Miss Kelly in the characters of Toupet and Cerisette. This sort of contrast was essential to an Adelphi drama; and in all such pieces Wright, Paul Bedford, or Toole, were expected to take an important part in the conduct of the story.   Indeed, it might be said, that in real life scenes of agitation and horror often engender grotesque situations and humours, which in their turn add a poignancy to the tragic elements.   In its new shape, therefore, the play seemed to present too much unvaried sadness, "an inspissated gloom," as Johnson calls it.*

* Mr. Coleman, who had secured the "country rights" of the piece, relates, in his interesting book, one of those tragic incidents that have often occurred behind the scenes—

"At our last rehearsal at the Gaiety Theatre, Glasgow, the Prologue had gone without a hitch, and we were all ready for the Taking of the Bastille, when a wait occurred in arranging the

The production of "The Dead Heart" furnishes
one more instance of the tact and abilities which
have secured the manager of the Lyceum his
high position.   Mr. Irving, seeing that there was
dramatic life and situations, brought the whole into
harmony with the times, and imparted to it a
true romantic grace.   It is admitted that he himself has rarely been fitted with a part so suited to
his genius and capacities, or in which he has roused
the sympathies of his audience more thoroughly.
It is only the romantic actor that understands what

scenery.   The delay appeared interminable, and everything was
in a muddle.

"'Now then, Mr. Brown,' said I, addressing the master
carpenter, 'are we to wait your good pleasure till it's time to
ring up?'

"Stirred to action, the man caught hold of a piece of scenery
he had been pointing out to his men, held it for a moment, re-
linquished his hold, threw his hands in the air, staggered, and fell
back heavily on the stage.

"My first impression was that he had been partaking too
copiously of 'the wine of the country;' but, on looking closer at
him, I saw he had fainted.

"Unloosing his neck-cloth, I gave directions for his men to
carry him down below the stage to the carpenters' shop.

"As they removed him, a vivid ray of sunlight from a
window at the prompt side of the stage fell upon his face, and
Miss Barry, who was standing beside me, grasped my arm, as she
exclaimed, 'Look, look!   My God, the man is dead!'

"'No, no.   I can't—I won't believe it,' I replied.   Then,

might be called the *key* of a play. We have plenty of effective, strident performers who would have presented Robert Landry as the robust opponent of tyranny—defiant, and, towards the close, pitilessly revengeful.

The moment when a popular actor enters on the scene reveals in a significant way the mystery of his attraction and his power. The stage is full of crowd and bustle ; there is a *va-et-vient* of glittering dresses, with a sort of histrionic turmoil. Of a sudden the inferior players relax in their well-meant, over-earnest efforts; the throng parts, and an obtrusive figure makes its way quietly to the

sending messengers in various directions for a doctor, the manager, and some brandy, I rapidly followed down below.

" When the brandy came, I tried to pour some down the poor fellow's throat—in vain, it came back again.

"Presently the doctor arrived. Feeling his patient's pulse, and placing his hand upon his heart, he bluntly said—

" ' Humph ! Stoppage of the heart. Dead !'

" The play had to be produced at night, and it was noted as a strange, ghastly coincidence that, when his friends and fellow-students were drinking his health, and that of his beautiful bride, when all was mirth and jollity, Le Grand brusquely exclaimed, ' Robert ! you remember Pierre Bastin, the carpenter of the Faubourg St. Antoine ? Well, *he died this morning !* ' At these ominous words a thrill went through every one on the stage, a pall fell over us, and we danced our sprightly gavotte as if it had been a funeral march."

and as for your son, that "Mighty hunter",
I beg to assure him that, in spite of my
talk about foxes, ~~when~~ as I sit here
before a field of white paper and hedged
in by books my only racing is confined
to my pen and, whenever I have a
nightmare in the shape of hunting,
it takes _this_ form

front to be greeted with a roar of welcome. There is, of course, some art in making this official *entrée* effective ; it can be, so to speak, "staged" like other scenes, and the ordinary "star" actor takes due care that the business of the moment shall be suspended, and that his followers are suitably grouped.

With the romantic, sympathetic actor, however, it is different. With him the most effective *entrée* will depend on the situation, and is unobtrusive. There is a significance in the face, the bearing, the fashion in which he even wears his clothes— accidents which *act*, as it were, and are a depart-ment of expression. The "reception" appears, as it should be, an involuntary interruption ; the play is still going on. His fellows, with voice and gesture, are importunately emphasising their pro-ceedings, more or less declaiming to the listeners— much more rather than less—what they have to repeat ; whilst he, with a strange magnetism, affects all by his "grace"—the mysteriously expressive face and bearing, and unexaggerated tone—so that when he is withdrawn for the moment, eyes are "idly bent" on such of " Nature's journeymen " as take up the business next.

The "Abbé," too, would have followed the imme-
morial precedent of the "crafty," insinuating abbés
who have so often figured on the stage.   The leading
"comique," who, in the remote performances, came
riding in on a cannon, ought to revel in his fooling
as a sort of revolutionary humourist.   But in the
late revival these things were softened and gradu-
ated as in a picture; some figures being merely
sketched, some put in the background, nothing
being intrusive.   By a sort of miscalculation the
style of one or two of the performers seemed hardly
in keeping: notably that of a sound, worthy actor, Mr.
Stirling, whose method belonged to an older school.
He seemed rather a blunt English sergeant of old
days, who had taken service with the French.   In
the same way, a nobleman of dissipated manners,
who attempted to carry off a young lady *à la
Richelieu* was portrayed by a performer who, both
in stature and manner, seemed to lack "dis-
tinction."   But these were slight blemishes, and
scarcely of the essence.

Irving's style—his excellences, as well as his
defects, are now familiar to all.   The last are
rather mannerisms, which, it has been contended,
are necessary attendants on every kind of excel-
lence.   The poet, the painter, and the orator

especially, has these personal peculiarities, which he, perhaps, regards with a tender allowance. Kemble, with all his gifts, was a serious offender in this respect; and his throat-clearings and his "aitches" were often the subject of good-humoured ridicule. In Robert Landry is exhibited no less than four contrasted phases of character: the gay, hopeful young artist; the terribly metamorphosed prisoner of nearly twenty years; the recently delivered man, newly restored to the enjoyment of life; and lastly, the composed revolutionary chief, full of his stern purpose of vengeance. This offers an opening for the display of versatile gifts, and were certainly brought out in the most striking contrast. But it is in the later scenes of the play, when he appears as the revolutionary chief, that our "manager-actor" exhibited all his resources. Nothing was more artistic than the sense of restraint and reserve shown, which is founded on a perfect knowledge of human nature. A person who has thus suffered, and with so stern a purpose in view, will appear disdainful of speech, and oppressed, as it were, with his terrible design. It is a common error that dramatic feeling must be expressed in words which may be illustrated by face and gestures; but it might almost be said that unvoiced expression is infinitely more telling and dramatic than any form of words. All through this portion of the play Irving's bearing and glances were in this spirit; his answers were made in this language. Quiet, condensed purpose, without any "fiendish" emphasis, was never better suggested. Even when the drop-scene was raised, and he was revealed, standing by his table, there was the same unrelenting mood, with an impression that here was one who had just passed through the fire, who had been executing an act of vengeance which had left its mark.

The crowd regard him with a strange awe and curiosity. In the duel, so quiet and deliberate are his offers of the passport, disguise, etc., that the audience for the moment was "trapped"; and when he at last unfolded his conditions and the price to be paid, a general rustle and wave of excited movement spread over all. During the combat, no less remarkable was his steady following of his adversary, his "holding him with his glittering eye"—like the Ancient Mariner—with all the certainty of destiny. This suggestiveness in tone and colour is one of the elements of romantic acting, and we would suggest that our actor might still further develop his resources in this direction. Mr. Bancroft, on the other hand, seemed to rely chiefly on the effect of his utterances, and such a part as the Abbé would bear "furnishing" to any extent in this "extra-lingual" direction. But it was a well-studied, solid piece of workmanship, notably in the later scenes, where there is a tone of haughty recklessness very happily conveyed.

Miss Terry, though fitted with a rather unpretending part, imparted to it, as was to be expected, all that bright *enjouement* and sympathetic grace which is her own and hers only. She is the romantic actress, alternately gay and pathetic, with that heartfelt earnestness which it is so difficult to present without affectation on the stage. Nor must we forget that popular favourite Miss Kate Phillips, who brought with her brightness and bustle.

As is well known, the manager is supported by a scenic artist of extraordinary ability, whom he has inspired by furnishing him with opportunities such as a scene painter could rarely hope for. The long series of Shakespearean and other dramas, each with its beautiful and original paintings, became a school. Experiments on the most magnificent scale were tried; and here the manager made his own inspiration felt to an extraordinary degree. The

lovely supernatural effects in "Faust" owed their
success to a novel and original use of what are
called "mediums," and which Mr. Craven has
utilised. These devices, as commonly used, suggest
the magic lantern, but at the Lyceum there is a
richness of tone and a fine mystery which lifts it
above vulgar associations. We venture to say that
nothing so beautifully suggestive, as well as
effective, has been seen on the stage as the last
pictures of "The Dead Heart."

There is a darkened chamber in the prison
whence Landry goes forth to make his sacrifice, the
meeting of the mother and son following. After
an interval the background lightens, and a misty
vision is seen behind, of the tumbrel moving on
the guillotine, and the admirably-posed figure of
Landry standing erect. To most spectators this
seemed to be the fitting and sufficient conclusion.
But what followed was a true surprise. With a
fine, almost imperceptible, progress, the background
seemed to dissolve, leaving "not a wrack behind;"
figures began to grow and multiply, a sort of lurid
tone came over all, and there was revealed the
whole scene of the scaffold, with—most effective of
all—the long row of revolutionary soldiers ranged,
their backs to the audience. This living shadowy

This is the only "dear stalking"

permitted. Yours truly
Watts Phillips

City afar off. Of late, owing to the
charming weather, I have been watching
it after this fashion.

DOSE

barrier between the reality and the visions seemed wonderfully effective. There was nothing of the usual pretentious "tableau" in this; the idea was conveyed that this scene was before the mind of the mother and son, which, in those high-strung, nervous days it might well be. The judicious *reserve* of the whole change, and the perfect repose, made it almost a dreamy intellectual operation, contrasted with the usual upheavings and "clatterings" with which such things are usually done.

In a drama like "The Dead Heart" music forms a fitting accompaniment, furnishing colour and appropriate illustration. It is almost uninterrupted from beginning to end. Mr. Irving has always paid particular attention to this dramatic element, and has called in the aid of composers of eminence, such as Mr. Hamilton Clarke, Sir A. Sullivan, and Sir Julius Benedict. The beautiful music to the "Merchant of Venice," by the first-named composer, will be fresh in our recollection; and that of Sir A. Sullivan to "Macbeth" has already found its place in the concert *répertoire*. M. Jacobi, of the Alhambra, furnished some effective, richly-coloured music to "The Dead Heart," alternately gay and lugubrious. More, however, might have been made of the stirring

" Marseillaise," which might have been treated in various disguises and patterns as a sort of *Leitmotiv*, much as Litolf has done in his symphonic work on the same subject, or as Schumann has treated it in "The Two Grenadiers." M. Jacobi, however, caught perfectly the feverish, agitated spirit of the time.

CHAPTER III.

AFTER a visit to Edinburgh, where he busied himself with some illustrations for Charles Mackay's " Whiskey Demon," he found his way back to Paris to plan new dramas. He later gave a graphic account to his friend Coleman of his intimacy with the elder Dumas, Victor Hugo, Gambetta, and others. In these *coteries* the young Englishman seems to have been cordially welcomed.

Soon after the production of " The Dead Heart " I went to Paris, partly to represent Webster's interests, partly as correspondent to the ——; but principally to perfect myself in the art of dramatic construction.

I took as my model Eugene Scribe and glorious old Alexandre Dumas. Did I know him? Rather! He was the most generous, large-hearted being in the world. He also was the most delightfully amusing and egotistical creature on the face of the earth. His tongue was like a windmill—once set in motion, you never knew when he would stop, especially if the theme was himself. Many and many a time have I sat into the wee small hours, a rapt listener, as he compared his youthful trials, troubles, escapades and *bonnes fortunes* with his trusty comrades—

Boccage, Macquet, and Frederick — the great Frederick Lemaître.

I suppose he must have been great in his time ?

Must ? He *was.*

Ah, well, when I saw him he was a hoary ruin—majestic in decay. When sober—which was not very often—he was moody and saturnine; when mellow, delightful; when drunk, mad. The first night of "Toussaint l'Ouverture," Lamartine's play, he was a howling maniac.

To return to Alexander the Great. Of course he had lots of fellows to help him in his work. He gave me a turn now and then, but Macquet was his right hand. He was almost as great a genius as his master. Dumas detested description and elaboration, but he would invent a plot in five minutes, and knock off a play in five hours, if the fit took him. He always maintained that he was a dramatist, and nothing more.

I made Dumas' theory my dominant idea of character and composition, as you will see in "Lost in London" and "Marlboro'." Ah! you don't know them—more's the pity. In "Lost in London" there are only two men and one woman. In "Marlboro'" there's only handsome Jack and the duchess; but, oh! such parts.

Those golden days and roseate nights in La Belle Lutèce were the happiest I ever passed. We've nothing like it here; we are all so confoundedly insular and insolent. From the first I believed in Gambetta. I always said he'd be a great man even when he "dried up" over his first brief in 1861, and it was at his express invitation that I went over in '68 to hear his defence of Charles Delescluze. Yes, my boy, I heard the Baudin speech—the speech which sounded the death-knell of the man of December and the

My dear Mr. Milbank

Mr. Watts Phillips and myself accept your kind invitation with pleasure Shall we say Wednesday 2 o'clock?

gang of knaves and thieves, pimps, panders, and cut-
throats who had enslaved and degraded France.

Here is a lively sketch of his manager, Webster :—

During my stay in Paris I wrote a lot of plays for
Webster, which are still lying idle, and likely to remain so,
since he will neither act them himself nor allow any one
else to do so. *Par exemple,* there is Job Armroyd in " Lost
in London." This play has been announced any time for
the past five years, but it has been put off from time to
time. Now he tells me he has dreamt that he is going to
die while acting the part, so the production is postponed
sine die.

Then there's my biggest play, " Marlboro'," has been
shelved for years—that's the part for you, my boy—but, of
course, I can't withdraw it, because he has paid for it.
Besides which, he took me by the hand at first, and has
been so kind ever since, and we have had such good times
together.

He often came to see me in Paris, and it was one
perpetual holiday. He is a wonderful man—never means
to grow old, and doesn't know the meaning of a headache
or of fatigue: never turns in till two or three, and turns
out again at eight as fresh as a daisy. Then his strength is
prodigious for a man of his age.

You should have seen him at the last carnival. A
great hulking bully of a Pierrot kept following and insult-
ing us. At last he laid his hand on Ben's shoulder. It
would have done you good to have seen the old boy
take hold of the hound and throw him over his head

E

like a feather. He didn't molest us any more, I promise
you.

These times were too bright to last.

He had speedily prepared a new drama—or
rather a series of dramas; indeed, from this time
his exuberant brain seemed to teem with scenes
and plots and whole plays, which he was ready
to supply with an amazing fertility. Prolific
writers, as they are called, must live in this
" superfœtation of ideas." There is a positive
delight and enjoyment in the exercise of the
imagination : one plan is no sooner conceived, than
it engenders another ; and the last is best of all.
On the other hand, the sluggish writer has many
a heavy hour: his composition is a painful and
laborious process, and too often reflects the
process of "its unkindly engendure." " The Curse
of Gold" was the first result: but was not found
acceptable at the Adelphi. The manager had just
engaged those delightful comedians—Wigan and
his wife—whose styles were so contrasted, and
who required to be nicely and accurately fitted—
and the ready pen of our author supplied what
was desired in the shape of a comedy called
" Paper Wings." The manager had also " commissioned" an historical piece in four acts, of

which the era was to be the 'Forty-five. He was also busy with long serial stories for Mr. Maxwell, and for papers like the *London Journal*.

" The proprietor," says Mr. Coleman, " was my good friend, W. S. Johnson, the *doyen* of theatrical printers, the manager, Mark Lemon, through whose friendly offices Phillips was placed upon the staff. Amongst his colleagues were Sir John Gilbert, who did the illustrations, and Charles Reade, whose ' White Lies,' strange to say, proved to be the most disastrous ' ventilator ' the paper ever had.

" Phillips's *nom de plume* on these occasions was Fairfax Balfour. Upon calling one evening, I found him actively engaged in the weekly instalment of a blood-curdling romance, entitled ' Nelly, or the Companions of the Chain.' Dinner was nearly ready, but the ' devil ' was waiting below for copy.

" ' The villain has hocussed Nelly,' said his amanuensis. ' What am I to do with her now ? '

" ' Why, rescue her, of course.'

" ' But how—how ? '

" ' Well, Algy comes on.'

" ' But he can't. The door's locked.'

" ' Well, he must burst it open.'

" ' He can't; it's barred and bolted.'

" ' Well, then, he must come over the tiles, through the window. Then a struggle for life and death. He upsets the lamp; it sets fire to the place : smoke, flames, all *the rest of it*. While the devouring element enfolds its victims and death on a pale horse rides on the blast. To be continued in our next. Don't forget the pale horse. That will do.' "

E 2

The writing of his comedy took him just a month—as he said, " It's hard work—night and day." But as usual, the comedy was to bring him trouble and anxieties. The Wigans were *difficile*, not to say crotchety. Of his various distresses he gives this picture, in a letter to his family, dated February 10, 1860.

First and foremost I have finished " Paper Wings "; I leave you to guess with what work (three acts in less than one month) ! The comedy is witty, sarcastic (very), and a good plot; but I have had a most terrible bother with the Wigans, especially Mrs. Wigan. They have thrown every *possible* obstacle in the way of its acceptance. Webster received the first act, and was " delighted "; then came a letter, " if so-and-so is not altered, *they* will not do it," etc., etc.—with an encouraging private note from Webster— " the fact is, that they have another piece of Taylor's, and will throw you over if they can. Taylor would willingly see you shut up for daring to come between the wind and his nobility. Pray mind your P's and Q's, *you've a lot to fight against*, for, I am compelled to give way if Wigan insists, as right of choice, in part, rests with him."

A pleasant feeling this, to work day and night with; but I pushed on, knowing that Webster would do *his* best to take the piece. Yet, as he owned, the obstacles against me were great, viz, a " *fixed* determination to object " on the part of the great actor (and Wigan *is a very great actor*) *before he had seen a line* of the piece.

Eden - bridge !!! Kent   *Jany 15th/7*

"Over the way a wagon   thinking
stands with six smoking horses, shrinking
while in the George and Dragin
The man is keeping himself dry - and drinking"

Eden (?) Bridge.
Kent
Jany. 24th

My dear Mr. Milbank
Permit me to call your

Then the second act was completed — verdict of
Webster "I think it capital, brilliant writing, and most
effective situations." I did work on, and on the 3rd finished
the third act, though very unwell both in eyes and
head.

To-day I have received Webster's letter, "I've had a
terrible time of it.—The W.'s objected to everything bit
by bit, till I lost temper and said, 'I won't take anything
of Taylor's, at any rate.' Then it was agreed it should
be read before the company—I read it, and it went off
triumphantly. *Even then* they declined it, unless I would
make their engagement twelve weeks, instead of six. I
have submitted, and so they act the piece. If it don't
turn out well, I'm done." This is *all* his letter, and I am
anxiously waiting more information.

Then referring to his story, he adds—

To make my peace of mind quite complete, I've quar-
relled with ——, refusing to continue the story unless
the character of the periodical is changed. Webster's
christened it "The Family Washtub." —— threatens *law*
if I don't fulfil to the letter my agreement.

My name is getting up rapidly in England. In the
Standard of last Thursday week they placed me as a
dramatist in the *first* place; and in the *Morning Post* "to
our rising young dramatist must be awarded the laurel."
But "my precious eyes," how they *all*, from Webster to
——, praise my novel. I *dare* not tell you what they
say, excepting that it ought to be in *Blackwood—then* it
would make my fortune.

There is only one bit of news that consoles me for much
care. The man *I* love best in the world, Nathaniel

Hawthorne, is about to publish a new novel. God bless him. *His* worst—"Blythedale Romance"—is better (in *poetic* thought) than anybody else's.

The captious objections of the Wigans were offered to the very last, bewildering the author. But the hearty encouragement of the manager all through supported him. As he wrote to his family in his own natural style—

Sincerely his estimate of me and the piece is higher than my own. I have, through the haste and bother, only a confused notion of what it is all about. They "poked me up" every day almost, and I scuttled on. I *know I strengthened Plynlimmon,* but it's "allus a muddle." What makes me so nervous is Webster's anticipation for the assistance a *second* success will be to our forthcoming spectacular, etc., etc., drama. Could he have kept on "The Dead Heart," he (Webster) says he should have cleared a *large* sum. Last *Thursday* they hadn't room for "half a man more in the house." Notice the *audience* for me this time. Webster thinks the Adelphi patrons are getting more intellectual. I have great *fear* of a *first* night not at all supported. Your letter gives me a *leetle* comfort—but, still I think you're both mistaken up to a *certain* point.

My blood be upon your head!

Webster *is* a fine-hearted noble fellow.

Thine—WATTS.

At last the comedy was produced: on the night

of February 27, 1860, some three months after the
appearance of " The Dead Heart." *

The author, unhappily, could not be present at
the performance, and, as on the former occasion,
had to remain in Paris.   His friends sent him
comforting telegrams, "Great and genuine success:
enormous house, and mostly a paying one, to the
roof crowded."   By a mischance—torturing to an
author—the wires had been broken by a storm,
and the message was fourteen hours on the road.
The criticisms were cold and carping.   No doubt
there was some jealousy of a young and *absentee*

---

* Here was the bill :—

PAPER WINGS.

BY WATTS PHILLIPS, ESQ., AUTHOR OF "THE DEAD HEART,"
ETC.

Characters.

Sir Arthur Plynlimmon (*aged forty*) .		Mr. Alfred Wigan.
Mr. Jonathan Garraway (*aged forty-five*)		Mr. David Fisher.
Sir Jacob Pantile .	(*Directors of* .	Mr. Paul Bedford.
Colonel Batter .	*the Gt. Mael-* .	Mr. Howard. .
Mr. Alderman Fungus	*strom Bank*) .	Mr. R. Romer.
Transfer . .	(*Stockbrokers*) .	Mr. Stuart.
Coupon. . .		Mr. W. H. Eburne.
Scrip . .	. (*Transfer's clerk*)	Mr. A. Powell.
Owen Percival	. (*Secretary to* .	Mr. Billington.
	Garraway)	

writer, who appeared to have a monopoly of one theatre. The manager wrote—

I hope you received the telegram, and that it enabled you to sleep sound. It was a genuine success, but the Press are most ungenerous, though they cannot deny the fact. The *Daily News* is an honourable exception, which I enclose, though I presume you will have seen them all. Oxenford went out, stating his delight, and then tried to knock the piece over this morning. The tone of the papers, I fear, will seriously injure us. They say S—— wrote the *Daily Telegraph. Nous verrons!* The *Sunday Press* are no great friends of yours.

Webster may well be astonished (wrote the author to his family) at the comparatively cold tone of the papers.

William Kite, Esq.	. (*of Falcon Hall, Surrey, better known as "Accommodation Bill"*)	Mr. J. L. Toole.
Flimsy	.	Mr. Charles Selby.
Mr. Hammer. . . (*an auctioneer*).		Mr. J. C. Smith.
Jones . . . . (*potboy*) .	.	Miss Stoker.
Servant.	.	Mr. Page.
Electric Telegraph Boys. . .	.	Misses Foote and Hayman.
Stockbrokers.	. .	Messrs. Morris, Conrai, Le Barr.
Mrs. Wylie . . . (*a widow*)	.	Mrs. Alfred Wigan.
Blanche Plynlimmon . (*aged eighteen*).		Miss Henrietta Sims.
Madame Kalydor ("*Nature's soft nurse*")		Mrs. Chatterley.
Tawdry. . . (*Mrs. Wylie's maid*)		Miss Kate Kelly.

Time—The Age we live in.

Sala declared loudly that he'd never believe W. P. had so
much wit in him, adding it must have taken me months.
Tom Taylor and a host of authors were there—"all," says
my informant (a literary man himself) "very highly
amused, *and ashamed to be seen so.*"

I cannot help smiling at what the critics say about
" carefully prepared dialogue," and most patiently " polished
epigram," when I think of my helter-skelter writing,
scarcely pausing for my meals, till my system has had
quite a shock.

I should like to hear how the second night and the
third night went, whether there was a call, etc., etc. Can
you learn ? Yates has been *very* kind in the *Daily News.*
Webster is coming for a short time to talk things over ;
then he acts " The Dead Heart " at Glasgow, Edinburgh,
Bristol.

The engagement of the Wigans, made long
before, had, as we see, interrupted the run of
" The Dead Heart," an incident familiar to
managers and always exasperating. This feeling,
however, is contingent on the success of the other
substituted piece; if all goes well, there is not
much to be lamented.

Webster says, had it not been for this unfortunate prior
engagement of the Wigans, he should have been clearing
nightly a large profit from " The Dead Heart." The whole
time of its run he had not one bad house, and his revival
of it for one night crowded the theatre to the roof.

The Queen desired her great satisfaction to be expressed

regarding the drama. I thought of writing her a line asking if there were any little office vacant about the Palace that she thought I could fill—for instance Comptroller of the Maids of Honour—but it might offend Webster, so I shall remain in obscurity, with modesty, as ever, my stumbling block. Webster, during the Wigans' engagement, produces "The Dead Heart" in the provinces. May it bring grist to his mill, for he is a rare good fellow! Let me have the weekly papers, they are so very important, and I paste *all* into a book—my lesson book, I call it, with lots of birch.

Our indefatigable author, now busy with new ventures, accepted the rather chequered fate of his drama with equanimity.

If there are leaves of laurel in the crown there are also plenty of thorns. Webster says the Wigans will *never* draw at the Adelphi. I am racking my brains over the forthcoming drama (Jacobite period, time 1745), and Webster is very urgent I should push on. Scene *must* be in London. Smith wants a piece for Dillon, but I shall stick, *true as steel*, to the firm friend who has never swerved from his faith in me. He had, as he wrote to another, a great many communications to reply to, that were forwarded by *friends* who *grow* with the success and expire with the defeat: a crop of social fungi engendered by sudden heat acting upon a damp, *close* soil. Now, having relieved myself of the immense burden of recognition to them, I get into a fresher and more congenial atmosphere, and after wiping my hand carefully, extend it cordially and gratefully to you. Deeply I am

"Cure for bad legs! Blessed, if I don't
have a pot, for mine is precious bad'un"

What, wonderful fellows these Uhlan
are..! they seem to carry the

with the... wherever they go

obliged for the trouble you so cheerfully undertook. Oxenford *expressed* his "delight," and then wrote a cold notice in the morning. Yates wrote me that it went "tremendously," objected, as you do, to Mrs. Chatterley, but said "it was a success that no one can deny." His notice in *Daily News* was very favourable. Wigan has written a jolly, complimentary letter, hoping that he may have the opportunity of carrying out many more of my conceptions, and desiring that our acquaintance shall become of a closer kind.

There is some ruefulness in all this, which seems to betoken that comfortless form of success—one of "esteem." It is pleasant, however, to note the cordial, kindly efforts of such friends as Mr. Edmund Yates. But the official judgment of other critics, like the late Mr. Oxenford, are not to be presumed from casual, good-natured utterances in the lobbies. This critic, with whom "first-nighters," as they are called, were long familiar—the only one of his order privileged with a box—was, it is notorious, almost too easy and indulgent, and often saw good in what was but indifferent.

He was now gratified by many offers from managers, and by commissions. He was approached by that eccentric specimen of an *entrepreneur*, Mr. E. T. Smith—who was perhaps the first in our time to introduce the purely commercial element into his calling, "running" a theatre very much as he would a shop. This was not surprising, as he had learnt his business at the "Royal Property," or Vauxhall Gardens, which he had administered in a showy and successful style.

E. T. Smith has written to me for a three-act drama to be put in hand immediately, Beverley to paint the scenery, and he will engage what principal actor or actress I can point out. Also, that if I can make an appointment, he will come over to Paris himself to arrange. All this I am forced to decline. Webster has commissioned a new four-act drama, and I must not, for any temptation, act unjustly to him. In his case, my word must be my bond.

He was more gratified by a friend's proposal to prepare for the French stage a version of his "Joseph Chavigny." But no poor hard-working *littérateur* ever encountered so many awkward checks and disappointments. His friend Webster, then in Paris, entered one morning with the news that he had just seen a piece called "L'Escamoteur," in which he had recognised his old friend "Chavigny." The author, being busy, thought lightly of the matter; but presently arrived the translator himself, in much alarm, who confirmed the news, on which both went off to see the piece, and found that it was the work of that most skilful of playwrights, D'Ennery, the author of the "Two Orphans," who had annexed the leading incidents. On this discovery the plan was abandoned. He had on hand, however, another more ambitious scheme—a five-act piece founded on the story of " Theodora: Actress and Empress,"

which abounded in spectacular effects, has "situations" of the Hugo and Dumas sort—is entirely original— and affords scope for marvellous beauty of scenery and costume. Miss Cushman was so taken with the "plot," etc., which we used often to talk over together, I altering much at her suggestion, that she gave it to Charles Matthews, who spoke in high terms, but walked off to "Ameriky," and it was with difficulty Miss C—— got back my MS. She wished me, at that time, to show it to various managers, and state her desire to act the part; and, that so high was her opinion of the play, that she would accept sharing terms on speculation of its success. But I, being then entirely unknown, except as a caricaturist, made at that time no further step in the matter excepting to lend it once to Miss Glyn for perusal, whose verdict was highly flattering, and dropped it into my desk. Webster read it, and thought it promised an enormous success, but owned it wouldn't do for him because the character was one for a *great* actress. Kean would have done it, but it was his last year at the Princess's, and he could not afford to make that a year of other than reproductions; *his* opinion was *most favourable.*

Phelps liked it; but objected that *his part must* top Theodora's. This was the play of "Hamlet" with the part of

Hamlet omitted with a vengeance, and I told him so. Miss Glyn was anxious I should write it, but could not afford herself to speculate. And there the business dropped. Since that time I have produced three dramas, and am in a *very* different position. It's just the piece for Drury Lane. Webster is very much taken with the characters of " Theodora," and thinks it will be a tremendous hit.

As regards the " Theodora " MS. my movements are, as yet, quite undecided. Webster seems to consider that until I have given him a second "Dead Heart" I have no right to do anything dramatic for anybody else. This is not quite my view ; but he is coming over to Paris to spend a few days with me, and the whole business will be gone into. He'd be glad to get off any further engagements with the Wigans (I imagine). *Comedy* won't do in a theatre which aims at being the " Porte St. Martin " of London. Should I make a move with " Theodora ? "

Such are the scraps of encouragement on which the sanguine dramatist feeds. But gradually there comes a change of humour ; the manager grows cold —the thermometer falls.

CHAPTER IV.

ON GHOSTS—A FILIAL LETTER—THE "'FORTY-FIVE."

HE was now offered the post of correspondent to the *Daily Telegraph*, which he declined from the good-natured motive that it would interfere with an engagement made with a struggling man, who he said "would starve" if he supplanted him. We find him also in consultation with Webster over a piece called "The Account Balanced"; and also still pursued by the lessee of Drury Lane with tempting offers. Yet though all this offered fair prospects enough, progress was but slow. For the working dramatist each play has but a precarious lot; may be "commissioned," yet found unsuited; may be accepted, and yet held over for years. Long and apparently satisfactory negotiation, with fitful turns, may lead to nothing in the end; or he may be invited to begin all over again, and supply something more suitable. These capricious changes have to be met with patience or fretfulness; and, what is more difficult, the spring and buoyant spirit must be maintained, or the work will be

indifferent.   No one encountered so much of this
as our dramatist; and it was not wonderful that at
times he sank into fits of despondency, from which
he suffered much.

Concerning your objection [he wrote at this time] to
the supernatural and utter disbelief in ghosts (though poor
Goldy says " appearances are in their favour "), I go half-way
with you only.· I *do* believe in a communion with this
world and higher intelligences; also in the union of
minds, or, how shall I term it? communion of spirit between those who loved sincerely and are separated.   I
believe in the possibility of that occurrence.   " The voice "
·that echoes through the heart of " Jane Eyre," as related
by Miss Brontë in one of the concluding chapters of her
strange great book,—I allude to the " cry " of Rochester,—
Mrs. Gaskell declares, on the word of C. B——, to be a
fact.   I *feel* the possibility of. such things.   But you
mustn't think that Goggs is the exponent of my feelings;
that gentleman, who, like Addison's old maid, is " always
seeing apparitions and hearing death watches, and was
nearly frightened into her coffin by the great house dog,
who howled in a stable at a time when she lay ill of the
toothache."
    Do you remember Addison's *beautiful* conclusion to
his essay on superstition?   I should like to get " Mr.
Stimpson's " and " Goggs's " opinion on it.
    " I know but one way of fortifying my soul against these
gloomy presages and terrors of mind, and that is, by securing to myself the friendship and protection of that Being
who disposes of events and governs futurity.   He sees, at

Agricultural Districts

What comes of reading the "papers"

"Let our peasantry get to study the daily press and all is well" John Bright

THE

RED COW

GIN

GOOD ALES

" You beant agoin in theer Giles? Whoi he be a Red cow !!! and Lunnon Doctors say he has gotten the scarlet fever !. "

one view, the whole thread of my existence, not only that part of it which I have already passed through, but that which runs forward into all the depths of eternity. When I lay me down to sleep, I recommend myself to His care; when I wake I give myself up to His directions. Amidst all the evils that threaten me, I will look to Him for help, and question not that He will either avert them, or turn them to my advantage. Though I know neither the time nor the manner of death I am to die, I am not at all solicitous about it; because I am sure that He knows them both, and that He will not fail to comfort and support me under them."

According to the testimony of his family, he was always deeply imbued with religious sentiment; though sentiment is of but little value unless fortified by practical acts. As Bishop Butler has so logically proved in the " Analogy," simple indulgence in pious sentiment actually enfeebles, if it does not destroy, the active principle.

Few men [writes one who knew him well] were quicker of temper, more bitter and sarcastic in anger—and very few were so ready to forget and forgive—save in one case, and *there* the injury was too great for forgiveness. Even when very young, he could never sleep after a quarrel with any member of the family, until there had been a reconciliation. His mother often related how, if he had had any words with his father, she always left the bedroom door unlocked, aware that he would make some excuse to enter, such as the borrowing of a watch key or th like

F

as he would never retire to rest until the little difference was settled.

This is a pretty trait, of a touching and rather
original kind, and betokens a really affectionate
nature.

"The Account Balanced" did not seem to suit
the Adelphi, and we hear no more of it. E. J.
Smith was still pressing for a work—and at last
received "The 'Forty-five" drama—which he appears to have purchased from Webster, and which
was in due course produced. It did not enjoy much
success. According to the late Mr. Boucicault's
sarcastic theory "Nothing could succeed at Drury
Lane"—at least in those days.*

In the next long, interesting, and most natural

---

* Here is the bill :—

"A STORY OF THE 'FORTY-FIVE."

An Original Drama in Four Acts.

Characters.

Sir Andrew Silverton　.　.　.　.	Mr. Webster.
Sir William Ashford.　.　.　.	Mr. Spencer.
Cyril Silverton .　.　.　.　.	Mr. MacLean.
Captain Hector Kilruddock　.　.　.	Mr. Farrel.
Evan MacIan .　.　.　.　.　.	Mr. Bedford.
Father Metzler. } *Jacobite Agents.*　.	
Chasseloup　.　}	

letter, addressed to his mother at Jersey, he out-
pours all his hopes, projects, and fears. There are
touches of buoyancy and despondency side by
side. It is dated 1861.

It seems an age since any communication has passed
between us, and I am longing to hear some news of you.
I have been laid up with a very severe attack of influenza
—brought on, I think, by the sudden presentation of a
doctor's bill for 4,000 francs, which I am vainly disputing.
I have been very ill, the recovery being all the slower
because I *persist* in sticking to my work. In another
fortnight or three weeks I shall have finished "Lost in
London" and commenced a new domestic drama, "*Something to live for*" which a French author has engaged to
translate as I write it, under the title of "*La vie ne vaut
rien sans elle*" or "*Rien sans elle.*" I am also slowly
laying the foundation of a new play, which will, I think,
stand quite up to the height of "The Dead Heart." It is
to be called "*St. Bartholomew's Eve,*" with the great

Enoch Flicker	.	.	.	Mr. J. L. Toole.
Sergeant Guffog	.	.	.	Mr. Paul Bedford.
Corporals Wotherspoon and Crick	.	.		
Bickers	.	. (*a drummer*)	.	
Tootle	.	. (*a fifer*)	.	
Landlord	.	. (*of Adam and Eve*)	.	
State Messenger	.	.	.	
Isabel	. (*Sir William's daughter*)		Miss H. Sims.
Jessie MacLeod	.	.	.	Miss Clyde.
Highland Kate.	*Rival Ballad Singers*		Miss Thirlwall.
Hanover Bess			Miss Howard.

F 2

gloomy figure of *Catherine de Medici* in contrast with brilliant tableaux, furnished by those terribly picturesque times. I imagine such a drama my speciality. I wish I could contrive to send you my MSS., but I can get slight information about Jersey *here.* It's looked upon as a kind of political outlaw's den ; hallowed, as all *thinking* people deem it, by the presence of that great Hugo, whose *name* is a talisman of power to move the heart of France.

I should like, if I can, to send my rough copy of 'Forty-five. *I* think it a far more talented play than " The Dead Heart." Also, I should like to forward " Lost in London " for your perusal. Can you give me any positive idea of the expense of such a parcel ? . . . , How I pray to get an *original* drama out here! If successful, it would make my fortune. ——'s influence is paramount at the Adelphi. Webster is old, and *very, very* shaky, and —— evidently hopes some day to become master of the theatre. . . . .

Boucicault writes me that *nothing* could succeed at Drury Lane—he foresaw it, etc. Webster says, innocently, " You've been *sold*, my poor boy ! I wonder they didn't bring it out at St. Paul's." I had two offers for the " 'Forty-five," one from the Princess', the other from Smith (manager of Drury Lane). I foolishly took the latter, Boucicault strongly advising it. . . . .

I had almost resolved upon visiting America next year, but this cursed split in the *dis*-United States has upset everything, and the Yankees are laying out their spare cash in bowie knives and revolvers. However, I shall keep my eyes open. It has been a hard time for me. I should have got a great pull if the " 'Forty-five " had been a success. *Yates* says it was a *great* success, but the *house*

45 Redcliffe Road
Bromfton Road.
(My Castle)

My dear Christine

I send this letter to you by a very old friend of mine. a Giant! but such a good fellow that, though he loves you so much that he could almost eat you up—he wouldn't hurt a hair of your pretty head. no—not for a hundred weight of Toffee or a ton of barley sugar

I Knew him when I was a little boy—such a little boy that I always went in and out by the Keyhole without opening the door. If you can go in and out of the Keyhole it is so much better you Know because you never leave the door open and dear mamma and papa will never catch cold—the only danger is that you might catch the Lock-jaw and that would be a Pity.

I was looking over my library the other day and found another book, the same I gave your big sisters. and I thought why shouldn't Christine have a set of Giants and fairies all to herself? To look over them in her own pretty way and talk of them in her own sweet fashion!

So, darling. I send you

the book — excuse my very short letter
because I am "greengaged" to a friend
and in a great hurry - but believe me
your affectionate friend and admirer

Master Watts

I am going to play a game
of hoop — Such Larks!

was a mistake. D. L. is *now* an opera and pantomime theatre, with now and then starring engagements for Kean and Brooke, but never for an original drama.

Celeste wants a drama—but what am I to do? I've sent a completed five-act drama in the rough, " The Half Brother " (an adaptation of " The Head of the Family "), to Webster, asking him to look over it; then, if he has no objection, I shall dispose of it to the Princess', who want a drama for Fechter, the French actor (the original Ruy Blas), who has made quite a sensation in London by acting in English. *He* stated he should like to have a play by the author of " The Dead Heart." But Webster's such a slow coach that he drives me frantic.

See how I work ! During the last twelve months I've produced "Paper Wings," three acts; " The Half Brother," five acts; " The 'Forty-five," four acts ; " Lost in London," three acts ; " Marlborough " (half completed), three acts ; and have in contemplation " Something to live for," three acts; "St. Bartholomew's Eve," three acts; "Breakers Ahead ! " two acts ; and all this with very indifferent health. Oh ! but for that one curse of my life ! Still, I shall conquer yet !

Answer my query about the MSS. *soon,* and believe me,

Your affectionate son,

WATTS.

Give my little man my best love and many kisses from his father.

N.B.—You say Blanchard had been asking about me. I wish you would learn *which* Blanchard ; whether it is my old friend, Edmund B., of Lloyd's paper, or E. L. B., the pantomime writer of D. L.—with exactly what they said. I feel sadly *your* absence from London.

If I can only get a success in this great theatrical and literary city, I could snap my fingers at London, that city of theatrical *barbarities*, in which "The Green Bushes" and such pieces are spoken of as those "great works."

A gentleman in the *Sunday Times* went out of his way to have a dig at me the other day in a notice on the "Colleen Bawn." "We've had enough of the intellectual school of writing, and do not hesitate to say that the 'Colleen Bawn' and 'Green Bushes' are far more amusing to an English audience—who go to be amused, not bored— than a dozen such brilliantly tedious productions as 'The Rivals' or 'School for Scandal,' even from tragic declaiming of such ambitious pieces as 'The Dead Heart.' 'The Wife's Secret,' 'The Duchess of Malfi,' or 'The Maid's Tragedy' (a good company) are more provocative of sleep than amusement. 'The Green Bushes' and 'The Colleen Bawn' are worth them all."

It is pleasant to think of this toiling, struggling man thus devoting time and zeal to entertain his family. At this moment he was almost overwhelmed with work, or rather with proposals and plans for future work.

I am likely [he wrote] to be *very busy*. Wigan (after applying in vain for my address at the Adelphi) has written to me haphazard for a something *à la Ruy Blas* for his autumn season. The letter he sends me is like himself, so gentlemanly, so business-like, and so true, that for every reason I am called upon to do my best, and so I shall. Great haste.

P.S.—I re-open letter to say that one has just arrived from Mr. Robson *accepting* the plot of "Married in Haste," and commissioning the comedy. "His Last Victory" has *been* read at the St. James' with *great acclamation ! ! !*

Of the Wigan proposal, however, we hear no more. He had also engaged in a co-partnership with Bayle Bernard, an industrious and now almost forgotten dramatist, to whom we owe "His Last Legs" and many an adapted melodrama. His buoyant ally speaks airily of "preparing several dramas" with his assistance. All the time he was living a gay Boulevard life, giving and receiving dinners—English friends, and friends of Webster's, constantly "turning up."

I understand there are some very fine contralto songs in the "Amber Witch." What do you think? Wallace *has had* rather a better success than the unfortunate Wagner. Such an audience! and such a sibilation! "Sindbad's Valley of Serpents" was nothing to it. But if the first night was noisy, the second night was quiet. A shower bath of poppy juice could not have produced a more somnolent effect. Indeed, one old gentleman was turned out by the box-keeper for snoring so loudly that he awakened the pit.

He also gives a sketch of the famous tumult when Wagner's "Tannhäuser" was first produced.

This combination of work and dissipation was beginning to tell upon his health, which from this time forth began to fail him. He in truth "lived hard" as it is called, and his labours were now interrupted by a sharp attack, which confined him to his room for some weeks. Still, his extraordinary spirit did not allow him to relax. He now engaged to write a new novel, and had just finished " The Foster Brothers," planned by Bayle Bernard, "but every line, nay, every word my own. Wigan and Harris both want pieces, and I have had a pressing order from the *Daily Telegraph* to take Horace St. John's place as leader writer."

But in many of these instances he had been too sanguine, and did not take into account the precariousness of theatrical promises.

CHAPTER V.

THESE checks and repulses are unfolded in another of his truly natural and affectionate letters to his mother—

April 7th, 1862.

MY EVER DEAR MOTHER,—In my long silence there has been no forgetfulness of you; on the contrary, every affectionate thought has been with you; but my battle, for the last three months, since my illness, has been a hard one, yet I have fought with courage and without defeat.

Yesterday saw the conclusion of my new comedy, "His Last Victory," which has been accepted by the St. James' Theatre, and I hope will prove the forerunner of other comedies, as it will if successful. Thus far my good fortune: now for my disappointments; they are great, as you will see. My new drama, "The Foster Brothers," which was, in part, accepted by Drury Lane, is, owing to Smith's sudden decision of closing the theatre till October, rendered unavailable in any way till that month arrives.

Disappointment number one. But disappointment number two is more serious, and fills me with a rage and

bitterness I will not venture to express. You know my
way of making out plots, in fact, giving almost the entire
piece in my plan. Well, for weeks I laboured on a most
magnificent plot, building it up *entirely* out of my own
brain. I called this drama (it's not a melodrama, but
a kind of "Lady of Lyons" play) "Married in Haste," and,
being applied to by Mr. Harris, the manager of the
Princess', for a piece for Fechter, sent him my detailed
plot. He was so pleased with its originality that he came
over to Paris and saw me about it. It was afterwards read
to Fechter, who refused it because the female part was so
strong. Harris wrote—" We all say that there is but one
actress in England who could do the part of 'Camilla
Hailstone' justice; that actress is Miss Amy Sedgwick."
Miss Sedgwick not being acting at the time, I thought
no more of it, but, with resignation gained by a thousand
misfortunes, put my piece away with a sigh. This took
place ten weeks ago. Last week I saw Miss Sedgwick had
been engaged by Robson at the Olympic, and remembered
my play.

I sent it in, and it was read *immediately*, for my name
now stands very high. Robson and Emden were charmed
with it, calling it a second "Lady of Lyons"; demanded
my terms for writing it, and all was on the very eve of
conclusion, when Robson chanced to tell the plot (for he
was much struck with its originality) to Miss Sedgwick.
She cried out in astonishment, "But the same plot, more
or less, was the subject of a little drama read to me last
week by Mr. Brougham (a friend of Fechter and Harris),
whose piece, 'Playing with Fire,' a translation from the
French, has been acting at the Princess', and in which
Brougham takes the principal character. The piece," she

The Last Rose of Summer

Sympathetic Butcher's Boy. "Well, Mister James, you do look as if you wanted a "pick-me-up."

James. "Nerves, all nerves! The Season has been too much for me, and, if our people aint off to the sea side this week, I throw 'em over. Iodine is what I want, Chops my boy! Iodine!"

said, " was evidently a hasty affair, but the plot, with a
certain alteration of time and place, is nearly identical
with Mr. Watts Phillips'." Upon which I received a
letter from the management begging an explanation, and
suspending all arrangements, because Miss Sedgwick
declined a part of such importance as mine, when there
was a little piece in existence turning on the same circumstances.

Of course I wrote to Harris an indignant letter, stating
that by his own avowal my plot was read to Fechter. But
while the plot was being read, Mr. Brougham was acting
in the theatre, and was, moreover, the literary adjunct
of the theatre. But Harris had himself suggested Miss
Sedgwick's name. Yet ten weeks afterwards I find a
piece, hurriedly written, has been presented to that lady,
with a plot in every way identical with my own. Such a
coincidence could not be *accidental.* My plot was com-
pounded from my own fancy with the exception of one
little incident, suggested to me by the correspondent of
the *Morning Post;* yet that very incident, all over a
cigar, is shadowed out in Mr. Brougham's piece.

I'll not bore you with what else I said, but I am not a
man to sit down tamely under an injury. You can imagine
what my letter was. " If," I said in conclusion, " my plot
has been purloined, I will not venture in a letter to say
what I think, but shall reserve that gratification till we
meet in public, when my expression will be worthy of such
an offence." Thus the matter stands, and I am waiting
anxiously for Robson's final decision, though I am afraid
Miss Sedgwick will refuse any piece to which " doubt " and
a quarrel are attached.

Is it not a misfortune? Their letter accepting my

piece was only a few *hours* in advance of the one retracting
for the reasons stated : the whole being doubly cruel when
addressed to me, who have always disdained to pillage even
an idea of another man's, but have acted with a scrupulous
honour in my literary career.   *Mais nous verrons !* *

* The following letter, written about this time to his sister,
will be of interest.

Written in a Volume of " Martin Chuzzlewit."

4, ELDON ROAD, KENSINGTON.

MY DEAR EMMA,—One of the most pleasing passages in
Scripture is that in which Christ, with a wisdom always divine,
speaks of the " widow's mite." It is with the same diffidence,
but also with the same feeling that beat in the heart of that
forlorn woman, that I make my little offering to you upon your
birthday. At present I am very poor, or, believe me, the gift
should have been very different, but, with all due respect for the
past, the value of a thing is *not*

. "Just as much money as 'twill bring,"

for neither of us, I hope, have yet to learn that the *motive* of the
giver is the *consecration of the gift*, and that

"Unselfish love may have the power
To make the meanest weed appear a flower."

If you already have the book, do not scruple to say so ; my library
is not a very large one—indeed, I carry most of it in my head
upon *wooden* shelves—but I daresay I can find another and more
fortunate volume to flutter its white wings and act as a messenger
of love between us.

God bless you, my dear girl, and may your 90th birthday find

"The Dead Heart" has been played by Webster at the Surrey, and is now at the Marylebone; this week, as announced, will make its 316th representation! He is going then through the principal towns. They talk about doing "Lost in London" this year. It was read, and the parts given out at last when I stopped it, warned by a kind friend that ——— (who dreads me more than ———) had cast it for the full blaze of summer. Miss Woolgar writes me that her part of *"Tiddy* Dragglethorpe" is the very best bit of Lancashire nature that she has ever read, and adds, "I will prove to you by my acting how much I appreciate the great part you have so kindly given me," continuing, "You, my dear sir, are *the* man who can smash this 'sensation' mania, in which the scene painter is the dramatist."

Nothing has vexed my vanity more, and may I say my love for you and my sisters, than the fact that you can neither see nor read my plays. For be it known to you, I am now quoted in the *French* as well as English papers, as the only original English dramatist. Bear in mind before you read "Lost in London" that it is pure Lancashire. I *studied* the dialect in Brayley's *Patois* of English Counties, then worked at Mrs. Gaskell and Miss Evans (glorious Miss Evans!), and afterwards a *highly-valued* friend made for me a vocabulary, and out of this grew Job and Tiddy. It

you as good and kind as your 19th, that they may say of you as Chaucer of that sweet Prioress—

"And all was conscience and tendre harte,"

nor *ever* outlive the belief that I am

Your affectionate brother,

WATTS PHILLIPS.

is Nature, if nothing else, and no man dare deny its *originality.* Again, *nous verrons.*

I've led such an attack upon the "sensation" drama; my letters under the C. D. appeared in the *Daily Telegraph.* I wrote one to the Proprietor privately (his son has just married Miss Webster), but, without consulting me, he published my letter and prayed for more. Again my vanity must speak. The letter was a great one, and poured into ———— as the *Monitor* poured into the *Merrimac.*

Patience! Only give me life, and with the help of God! I will be instrumental in "smashing" this sensation drama.

The awkward *contretemps* notwithstanding, Mr. Robson handsomely accepted "Married in Haste," and produced the piece, as will be seen further on, with unequivocal success. The indefatigable author was now, as he said, "loaded with work." Two pieces at the Olympic and St. James'. "Harris offers any terms for a piece, and Buckstone desires a comedy."

With the exception of the drama [he wrote to an old friend] written by me months ago ("The Foster Brothers"), *melo*drama and I have parted company for ever. Comedy and drama will henceforth be my speciality, and, as I look around at my desk covered with pleasant letters from both actors and managers, I feel that it is not only possible but probable I shall leave behind me a *name.*

I have neglected you, old friend; I have neglected

"Mamma! Isn't it fortunate that Baby is n't
so very, very, very little?"
"Why dear"
"Because if it were, papa would stick a pin
through its back and put it Under a Microscope"

Mr Greathable

August 1st

"all right! Doctor, I've
got him tight"

45
Redcliffe

BISMUTH

Road

every friend but my pen; to that I have stuck, and the
result has proved my wisdom. But now with the certainty
of remunerative and creditable work comes back the wish
to hear from and see if possible the friends I value—value,
indeed, too much to bore them with my troubles till I can
speak of my troubles as nearly past.

Come over here for a few days—I can manage you a
shakedown! and can assure you a most hearty welcome;
also can introduce you to very charming society. Come!
you will not regret your visit, and of one thing be always
certain, whether I am faulty in correspondence or no, that
there is no friendly voice I am more pleased to hear,
no jolly, friendly mug I am so pleased to look upon as
yours.

No less than four of these pieces, as he wrote to
his friend, "Fred" Jones, were pretty certain to
appear that year, "Married in Haste" at the
Olympic; "His Last Victory," at the St. James';
"Lost in London" at the Adelphi; and "The
Foster Brothers" at Drury Lane. It did not
seem to have occurred to him that the stage is not
exactly adapted for this sort of wholesale manufac-
ture. A play, like a statue in a public place, requires a
large area of observation; and the public attention,
always languid, needs pause and deliberation. The
attraction of a play has to sink in, and filtrate slowly.
In literature there are so many kinds of audiences
that a diligent caterer may be as industrious as he

lists; but the public, which has but one pair of eyes or ears, in the theatre, soon grows fatigued or bewildered, if its attention be distracted by a succession of dramas from the same hand.

In his letter he alluded to his attacks on a form of the drama then in high favour, and which he detested, naturally perhaps, because it was the destruction of his own free and natural style. This is what was called the "sensation drama," the introducer of which was Mr. Dion Boucicault. This ingenious, versatile man had been successful in all departments of the drama, from his early comedy, "London Assurance," to his famous Irish dramas, and the artificial and unhealthy "Formosa." At one time, "the water cave" in the Colleen Bawn, with the leap across it, were thought to be prodigies of "sensation," as well as the railway trains, and realistic pictures of London slums in his other pieces. These things would be smiled at in these days of Drury Lane triumphs of "The World," a "Million of Money," etc. The fact remains, however, that in spite of protest and ridicule, "sensation" has held its ground to the present hour, and materially affects the general course of the drama. As I have said before, this must be accepted as the result of the "form and

pressure" of the age ; it must be received, therefore, to a certain extent, as a legitimate development.

In June, on the 21st, 1862, "His Last Victory"
was produced at the St. James' Theatre.*

* The bill of the night was as follows :—

"HIS LAST VICTORY."

(*An Original Drama in Two Acts.*)

Characters.

General Hercules Lacroix . . .	Mr. George Vining.
Baron Horace de Fauconville (*forty years*)	Mr. F. Charles.
Felicien Doucet (*nephew of the General, twenty-eight years*) .	Mr. F. Dewar.
Copernicus Kopp	Mr. Ashley.
Molasse	Mr. W. H. Stephens.
Sergeant Pons (*servant to the General*) .	Mr. Garstin Belmore.
Phinucan (*a footman*)	Mr. Bayley.
Monton (*a peasant*)	Mr. Cockrill.
Octave Decourcelle ⎱ (*friends of the Countess*) ⎰	Mr. Lever.
Jules de Fayolles	Mr. Henry.
Volnay	Mr. Gordon.
Laborde	Mr. Meline.
Countess Beauregard (*twenty-five years*) .	Miss Herbert.
Julie D'Aumont	Miss Ellen Turner.
Madame Molasse	Miss Isabel Adams.
Madame Du Helder ⎱ (*friends of the Countess*) ⎰	Miss Phoebie.
Madame St. Roche	Miss Reynolds.
La Baronne D'Autin	Miss French.
Mlle. Melanie	Miss Cooke.
Mlle. Deschamps	Miss Graham.
Fichu (*the Countess' maid*) . .	Miss Lillie Lonsdale.

G

"Married in Haste" was now ready, and was produced at the Olympic Theatre on the 10th of November, 1862, under the altered title of "Camilla's Husband." * This was, perhaps, the most successful of his productions after "The Dead Heart," and owed much to the effective playing of Mr. Henry Neville, at that time peculiarly fitted by his person and "gallant" style of playing characters of romance.

This drama was dedicated to Henry Neville, and met with a very cordial reception from the

* The bill ran :—

"CAMILLA'S HUSBAND."

(An Original Drama in Three Acts.)

Characters.

Sir James Hailstone	. . .	. . Mr. James.
Sir Philip Hailstone	. *(his son)* .	. Mr. G. Vincent.
Sir Thomas Kendal	. . .	. Mr. Franks.
Major Lumley	. . . .	. Mr. H. Cooper.
Captain Shrimpton.	.	. Mr. H. Rivers.
Dogbriar	. .	. Mr. F. Robson.
Maurice Warner .	} *(Artists)*	{ Mr. H. Neville.
Hyacinth Jonquil .		{ Mr. W. Gordon.
Maybush	*(Landlord of the " Red Lion ")*	. Mr. H. Wigan.
Chowler	. . . *(A smith)* .	. Mr. C. Harwood.

Servants, gentlemen, villagers.

Lady Camilla Hailstone .	. . .	. Miss Kate Saville.
Lady Roseville	. . .	. Miss Grant.
Miss Placida Poyntz	. . .	. Mrs. Leigh Murray.
Red Judy	. . *(wife of Dogbriar)*	. Mrs. Stephens.
Slowberry	. . *(their daughter)*	. Miss F. Haydon.

The Noble Tartar

Voice " Dont move! dont move! (aside) If
you do, I bolt!.

My dear Tartar! my cream of all the
Tartars and chief of all the Tartar 'Orses!
I am going to make you a little present
our interviews have hitherto been but short ones
Tartar. I know you love me from the way you
always investigate the calf of my leg to see
if there is not yet some little meat there and
how the bone is getting on.
With this letter you will receive your
portrait framed and glazed! You'll not be offended
if I say you have an ugly mug Tartar, but there
are uglier mugs still manufactured in the
Potteries and many uglier dogs (though they
don't think it) in the photographer's windows –
besides, with you, like with Mirabeau, another
ugly dog, your ugliness covers a great soul.
Take my picture, Tartar, and show it
to

to your good master and missis, they will appreciate it for it is a fine etching, now rare and full of power

Give my love to your young master and your young misses and wish them a merry Christmas and the happiest of happy New Years

Good bye, old fellow! I was a jolly dog once, though somewhat of a sad one now, and if ever you see a stranger with a particularly long mug wandering Streatham way, look on his collar for the name of *Watts Phillips*

Tartaric Acid

"A custom more honored in the "breech" than the observance"
Shakespeare

December 22nd 1873.

public and the critics. Its poor author, however,
could not yet quit his enforced exile to witness the
performance. In the same year the Briarean
dramatist had a farce, also produced at the
Adelphi, " The Ticket-of-Leave," not the melodrama of nearly the same name, and which, in the
hands of Toole, Paul Bedford, and Mrs. Billington,
was perfectly successful. Toole as " Aspen Quiver "
was at his best, and is still fresh in the memory.
As the author wrote—

" The Ticket-of-Leave " was written five years or more
ago for Webster, but not produced. I suggested it for the
present time ; he jumped at the notion, and it has proved
a screaming success; and the acting-manager added,
" There's no mistake about ' The Ticket-of-Leave ' pulling 'em
in. We've empty house to the whole price, but good ones
to the half. The people scream with laughter ; and the
governor finds it the ' ticket,' and no mistake." So much
so that it is now played before the pantomime. " Camilla's
Husband " is a mighty success ; so much so that Robson
appears in no burlesque this year; the first time for many.
It's a Belgravian success, Wych Street being, they wrote
me, blocked up nightly with a line of carriages as in the
Vestris time. Alas ! it is not the author who gets rich.

We are almost bewildered in attempting to recall the profusion of pieces which were now being
poured forth from this busy pen. " Lost in London," so long deferred, put aside, and put off, was

G 2

now positively to be produced, as soon as Miss
Woolgar (now Mrs. Mellon) had recovered from
her illness. But the " unlucky piece," as the author
always considered it to be, was again postponed,
the reason being Webster's failing health. *En
revanche*, he was gratified by the production of
" Paul's Return," * which had almost the success
of " Camilla's Husband."

The success of these pieces, as usual, brought
the author fresh commissions, which, equally as
usual, the undaunted author accepted. Accordingly,
we now hear of " The Woman in Mauve" and the

* The bill ran—

"PAUL'S RETURN."

Characters.

Richard Goldsworthy	Mr. Vining.
Geoffrey Goldsworthy	. Mr. C. Seyton.
Howard Flyntskin .	. Mr. H. Mellon.
Paul Goldsworthy .	Mr. John Nelson.
Herbert . .	Mr. H. Forester.
Abel Honeydew	Mr. David Fisher.
Beeswing . .	. Mr. R. Cathcart.
Miss Zenobia Goldsworthy	. Mrs. H. Marston.
Mrs. Geoffrey Goldsworthy	Miss Caroline Carson.
Beatrice Goldsworthy .	. Miss Kate Saville.
Blanche Wilton . . .	. Miss Rebecca Powell.
Mrs. Clampit .	Mrs. Hill.

" Huguenot Captain." No wonder he wrote in June, 1864, that—

My notes are doomed of late to be short; I am so overcome with work that I have no time to write long letters. I hope, if I succeed in getting the original piece, " Jane Shore," I am preparing for Madame Judith (the first tragedienne of the Français), accepted in France, *as well as in England,** I shall be elected a member of the French Authors' Society, and then shall hope to write for the French stage as well as the English. Webster tells me that " Lost in London " is on the eve of appearing again.

But, as it proved, Webster failed in his promise, and the author was once more doomed to disappointment.

Sothern appears in my new comedy, " The Woman in Mauve," at Christmas, and is coming over next month to spend a few days with me *à propos* of a new idea of a great character for *him.* I have been very unwell. My frightful digestion! It has prostrated me for nearly a month, and literally incapacitated me from working at my plots and new ideas. However, I'm up and at my desk again— shaken in health, but, thank God, strong in heart, and never meaning to say die until the time comes.—Yours affectionately, WATTS.

Again, it may be noted how remarkable it is to find an Englishman thus winning fame in the rather

* This scheme, however, was never carried out, owing to a quarrel with the lady.

exclusive circle of French *littérateurs.* It will be
seen that he complains of illness; indeed, for the
future there was to be added to his heavy labours
the burden of struggling against disease. To find
inspiration for plots and characters when a prey to
headaches, indigestion, and pains of all kinds, is a
new suffering itself. But he surmounted all gal-
lantly. Fresh and yet fresh toils were imposed
upon him.

Thanks, and many thanks, for your kind letter, which
I will answer in a far more lengthy way ere long, but you
have no idea how much I am overworked. Thank God
the result will be apparent next year. Sothern has commissioned from me *three* original comedies, after having
read and refused manuscripts sent him by ——. The
compliment is great; the fame, if successful, will be immense; the mental work, work *awful.* Boucicault has
shelved, for a time, my drama' at the Princess', while poor
Webster's failing health shelves "Lost in London." My
new comedy, "The Woman in Mauve," *entre nous,* appears
next year at the Haymarket.

I've just come back from the great camp at Chalons,
where I was sent to write an article. I did expect to have
a three weeks' absence from Paris, and a free trip to Madrid
on the opening of the great railway that, passing through
the Pyrenees, connects Paris with Madrid; but illness has
prevented it, so another of the press-gang got the job of
describing the Iron Dragon's invasion of the heart of
romantic Spain. It was a great disappointment.

" As it used to was!:"
The delight of women and the envy of men!.

Very cumfy'!

Something the matter with the toes! Oh! you're beginning, are you?

Oh! pickles!!!!

Aren't you ashamed of yourselves?

I can't stand it! Send for Dr. Ord, He's my leg-is-a-Tde!

Oh!!! Heavens time to Mr. Phillips!

The only pupil of George Crook-shanks.

Dec. 31st /73

My dear Dr. Ord.

Oh! I have passed a miserable night, so full of neuralgic pains and ghostly dreams, that de tile ta "

I have comparative rest for days and then, suddenly my legs commence their acrobatic and most painful feats (I wish I had no feets!) till "laying aside my manhood as Rosalind says" I absolutely scream.

The opium pills I adore but I find no perceptible effects from the Belladonna in the shape of slaying pain.

Do you think you could add something to the enclosed

A new edition of All-of-a-twist (Oliver Twist)

I have been terribly worried by visitors to see me ; first Sothern for a month, then E. J. Smith for a piece, which he didn't get, then Bateman *père* for the drama of "Jane Shore," which he wanted to buy for his daughter. Then Henderson, the Liverpool manager, and now Webster's coming—all take up time. I'm afraid this is a very, very dull letter, but I am low-spirited from many causes. One, and the most immediate, is that a few hours ago I left the bedside of poor Vincent Wallace, who is dying *rapidly*, to my idea. We are very close friends, and I have been dishing into something like shape a portion of the new libretto sent him from London—of course *con amore*. I fear he will never live to compose another "Lurline" or "Maritana." His poor wife is in a sad way. I have asked his boys to spend the evening with Leslie; it will be a bad thing for them, W.'s death, though I suppose his family *must* get a good pension.

I am going to an immense party to-night—ambassadors, dukes, marquises, and all kinds of people to dinner. I wish I was *not*, for I feel both ill and weak; bed would be by far the more welcome place, but it's impossible to get off.

In the letter in which he speaks of "The Woman in Mauve," he refers again to his severe indisposition, being now under the advice of the Emperor's physician, Dr. Reyer, who seemed to have regarded the case most seriously. He concludes—

I eat little, and drink little, but find life after all a very poor and sad invention. So much for the muffled

bell. Now I will strike a gayer chord. It appears my
" Woman in Mauve " has been a most *extraordinary*
success in Liverpool. They wanted originality, and they've
got it, for the critiques declare that " such a piece has never
been seen before on the English stage,"; and Sothern says
that the astonishment and enthusiasm were wonderful. It
will be produced in about six weeks at the Haymarket, and
they expect it will take London by storm. We shall see—
the piece is certainly one of the most eccentric character.
The idea was knocked out one summer's evening, when I
was racking my brains as to what kind of sledge-hammer
blow *I* could strike at the giant Sensation. I wrote it in
great pain, and it contains jokes enough for six.

I have sufficient work before me for the next six
months if I have *sufficient* strength to get through it.
That is the great difficulty! Plays may send my name
up sky high, though possibly I shall be sky high also.

CHAPTER VI.

SOTHERN—"THEODORA," AND OTHER PROJECTS.

AT this time the attraction of Sothern, in his inimitable character of Dundreary, had waned; and he conceived the idea that he had all the necessary gifts for making a reputation, in parts of more pretension, and even in tragedy! In this curious delusion he persevered almost to his death, though the public always declined to accept him *au sérieux*. The lovers and chivalrous characters that he now attempted were poor performances: his voice even was inharmonious. Still his popularity was unbounded, and caused him to be accepted. A grotesque form of advertisement, probably of American origin, was adopted to introduce Watts Phillips' new piece at the Haymarket.

For some time there appeared on the walls and hoardings a huge poster representing a frame, with these words on a white ground " *Watch this frame !*" In due course the words were replaced by the title of the forthcoming drama, " The Woman in Mauve." It was produced March 18th, 1865, and met, like the later Sothern creations, with but moderate success.*

He was now engrossed with plans for bringing forward his old spectacular tragedy "Theodora," which had so long lain by him. We also find him busy with what was to be a favourite project with him for many years—a drama on the subject of "Marlborough"—and which, like most of his favourite projects, he found perpetual difficulties in getting appreciated. Such a subject, indeed, seems likely to have been of a rather stilted kind.

A letter to him from his friend Webster is interesting, as exhibiting the depressing care and uncertainties of theatrical life, where nothing seems to go well, or steadily:—

KENNINGTON PARK,
April 2nd.

MY DEAR PHILLIPS,—I have been going to write to you

---

* The caste was as follows :—

Frank Jocelyn	*(an artist)* .	Mr. Sothern.
The Count .	. .	. Mr. W. Farren.
Launcelot Harvey	*(a surgeon)* .	Mr. Howe.
Beetles. .	*(a policeman)*	. Mr. Compton.
The Countess	. *(the Woman in Mauve)* .	Miss Edith Stuart.
Lucy Harvey .	. .	Miss Lovell.
Mrs. Mary Ann Beetles	.	. Mr. Buckstone.

My dear Doctor. Saturday June 7
— I have just cut the following
from the Daily Telegraph, and must send
it you

> A most determined act of suicide has been
> committed by a boy of fourteen, vexed at the
> imperfect fitting of a new suit of clothes.
> Having strapped his ancles together, he pro-
> ceeded to hang himself in such a manner as to
> suggest a thoroughness of purpose. &c &c

Master   Brummel
who   died
of   a
             fit—

Affliction sore, long time he bore
     He "tunded" was and hit—
But Master Snob could bear no more
     This most "uncommon fit"

     I had

every day, but I could hear nothing satisfactory to communicate. I have scarcely ever been outside this room since my return, for I have been very queer in health and worried in mind; for nothing is settled, nor does it promise a settlement.

If you had read the Friday's *Telegraph*, you would have seen that I was at the Fund dinner, though unexpected, and I should have been in for the "Drama," but escaped luckily with toasting only the vocalists. I met Dickens in the afternoon by accident, and he insisted upon my being present, consequently everyone now knows that I am in London, *to my cost*. I am smothered in letters, and my bell worn out with calls, so that I regret leaving Rue Lafitte. Unfortunately I had bad news from Wales on my arrival; I must go down there, but it will not, I fear, be a pleasant journey. Strange to say, the old " Wreck Ashore " is drawing money. We had a capital week last week, which is considered the worst in the year.

I saw Shepherd yesterday, and of course " Theodora " was uppermost. He says it will be well got up, and I have lent him the properties out of " Sardanapalus " from the Princess'. He wishes he could have afforded to spend more on it. He don't seem to know what " Avonia " will do with the part, but thinks she is not up to it. I believe, at least Gideon told me, they have been obliged to make two acts of one in consequence of the change of scenery, so it will be in six acts instead of five. Hingston having dropped his extra advertisements, Shepherd dropped his, so there has been no puffing for the last few days. Shepherd said that Hingston was going to do wonders with " Theodora "; but as yet has done nothing; only one bill with " Avonia Jones " in Greek. She has been receiving at the rate of

£100 per week, and says that does not pay her. I hear she goes to Australia from here, owing to Brooke's death. I will be at the first representation, and will write to Buckingham, or see· him. I had a long talk with Miss Glynn about "Marlborough." It seems she had consented to enact the Duchess which she said was very good in the two first acts, but fell off in the last. She said that Sothern could never have acted Marlborough, especially the last act ! and that she told him so. She could see me in the character, and should be delighted to be my Sarah.

Buckstone could not, he said, get his own part in Marston's comedy into his head. There was some difference of opinion as to its merits in the provinces. *Sothern must mind what he is about.* He is going to have another trial with the spirit-rappers.

Give my love to Mrs. Stirling, and pretty Mrs. Lee, and best regards to good old Whitehurst.

For yourself, you have my warmest friendship, and please God, St: Prix shall see me your guest, where I shall be at home I know and feel.

Yours faithfully,

B. WEBSTER.

This is an interesting letter from the worthy, sterling manager. But "Ben" Webster's own troubles were gathering about him. He was now, with his company, falling out of fashion—hanging " on a rusty nail." It is sad to think of the decay that overtook him and his friend Buckstone, both "lagging" somewhat ingloriously on the stage, and, in their decay, often to be seen hovering about the Café de l'Europe in the Haymarket.

As usual, all sorts of dreams and speculations as to his new favourite filled the dramatist's soul. Every one who read it was enchanted. He would take stock of his vast projects and of his numerous pieces, which

must some day be acted, and make me a name for a *tombstone. Why, there is a dramatic reputation itself locked up in a box.* It's heart-breaking! Webster has "The White Dove of Sorrento," "By the Sad Sea Wave," "Dr. Capadose's Pill," "The Half Brother," "Maud's Peril," and "Lost in London." Sothern has "Marlborough" and another *splendid* character piece, *and* a *drama!* D. B. wants comedy. Vining has two great *sensation* pieces *Ten plays!* All this besides my regular work, and the pieces now in hand.

Though requested to do it, I was from sheer break-down compelled to refuse to act as Paris correspondent for the *Daily Telegraph* for a month or six weeks last Christmas. They call me "Correspondent Unattached" to that paper, and nothing but necessity would have induced me to refuse to oblige people who have done me much good, especially as it is difficult to find persons abroad capable to write letters such as they require at a short notice. I did the September letters for the month, but couldn't do more from mere lack of time.

Sothern, *I* think, will not remain very long at the Haymarket—*nous verrons.*

QUITE BETWEEN OURSELVES. Phelps is charmed with

the part of " Marlborough," and is (this is PRIVATE) working heaven and earth to get it done, for Sothern, who is
my friend, will sell back the piece if other parties will
consent—but there is a certain fable called "The Dog in
the Manger." Phelps has just sent me his photograph.
He is much changed, but a splendid actor all say, and *my
man*—if we can work it—for the Duke. He says the
drama is admirable indeed—splendid *in all parts.* Again,
nous verrons.

Mr. Shepherd is coming over to stay a few days with
me next Saturday. I will see about Jefferson. Avonia
Jones, or rather Mrs. G. V. Brooke, was scarcely able to get
through her part. She had not eaten, she tells me in a
letter just received, since the news reached her of the
" London," and, to make her grief the more bitter, it was by
her *persuasion* that Brooke left earlier than he intended, to
arrange for her, and also by her warm persuasion that his
sister Fanny accompanied him. She is nearly mad with
grief, she says—grief and remorse. What a world of
sorrow it is ! Only a few months ago she was over here as
happy as a bird—if birds are really happy, with falcons,
hawks, to say nothing of sportsmen, hovering about them.

I have had to write to Fechter, who asserted (without
seeing more than the bills) that my "Theodora" was only
an adaptation from a piece called "Valeria." I have
written, and written sharply. D. B. said he knew the
drama was one whose name he'd forgotten, but Rachel had
acted in it. And Barnett, Lacy, Leicester Buckingham (so
Mrs. Brooke writes me) echoed this opinion. Pleasant,
when an author writes, with the most perfect *honour* and
trust, the words "entirely original" upon his piece, to
have even before production the contrary insinuated among

all the critics. However, I've been pretty plain. I assert my play is original in the fullest sense of that elastic word, and he who asserts otherwise is either a knave, a fool, or a liar—probably the three.

I'm sick of England and the English, and would give ten years of my life had I been born a native of this great nation of literature and art, rather than one of a people whose literature now is "robbery ill-concealed"; and, as every "author" has his hand in a Frenchman's pocket, he suspects the "originality" of everyone else. In France dramatists make fortunes in a few years, and, before a man has written half-a-dozen great pieces the cross of honour glitters at his button-hole. Eliza Cook was right, and if an Englishman is a dramatic artist "a flush should rise from cheek to brow as he speaks of his native *earth*."

May I be luckier with " Marlborough " (*that's* not likely to be French) and the " Huguenot Captain " ; the latter will be *splendid*.

Send me a telegram of the first night. I haven't, to my *knowledge*, one friend in the house, and it's the most important piece I have yet written. Shepherd refuses orders, save the few, saying, "the piece will play itself." So be it. Whatever the scenery may be, *I* designed it—*all of it*. They knew as much of the time as I do of Sanscrit. I have literally sketched all the dresses.

The piece was produced in due course, but with rather disheartening result. His friend Webster wrote him an account of the first performance.

April 14*th*.

MY DEAR PHILLIPS,—I have purposely delayed writing

to you, knowing that you would have lots of congratulatory letters from others.

Of course, I and my son Ben were all there the first night. There had been no stir made about the piece, consequently there was a bad house. I do not understand the change in the policy of Mrs. G. B. and Hingston, but they have absolutely let the piece down by want of the usual billing and puffing.

It went exceedingly well; not one note of disapprobation from beginning to end. It was badly acted in general, but the scenery and dresses were excellent. Mrs. G. B. had neither brain nor physique for Theodora. She looked uncommonly well in the first half-naked dress, but the best, and only good thing she did throughout the play, was where she sits on the throne "robed and crowned" to meet King Death. The consequence was that the *spectacle* overrode the dramatic element. The second night went much better, but she cannot touch the part. The fine scene was scarcely heard, and was an awful failure for you.

I send you two papers. *The Advertiser* also is good, but I could not get one. The infernal humbugging Reform Bill kept the notices out of some of the papers.*

---

* It would seem that to this spectacular piece the Theodora of the "divine Sarah" was somewhat indebted. The author—Sardou—addressed this letter to M. Mayer, of the *Gaulois*—

December 27, 1883.

Oui, mon cher Mayer, il y a une Theodora Italienne et une Theodora Anglaise, et de plus une pièce Français intitulée "L'Imperatrice et la Juive"; et j'aime mieux avouer tout de suite, fidèle à mon habitude c'est avec ces trois pièces que j'ai fait la mienne

Amitiés.—VICTORIEN SARDOU.

A few years ago, when M. Sardou's "Theodora" had been produced in Paris, Mr. Sala, in his "Echoes of the Week," recalled, in very kind terms, the "Theodora" of Mr. Phillips.

On receipt of a letter thanking him for his remembrance of his dead friend, Mr. Sala sent the following reply, which it is hoped he will not object to being reprinted here:—

38, YORK ROAD, BRIGHTON,
Friday, September 26th, 1884.

MY DEAR MISS PHILLIPS,

"Why cert'nly" I remember to have heard Watts talk of "Theodora," but I never saw the drama. Is it in print, and to whom does the copyright belong, I wonder? If Sardou's play is successful, it will surely be produced in this country; and—it would warm the cockles of my heart to incite some London manager to bring out a "native" version of "Theodora."

Faithfully yours,
GEORGE AUGUSTUS SALA.

The drama was [and is] in print—in the Lacy edition. In an interview with Mr. French he stated that the copyright was his; also that he was of the opinion that the expense of scenery, &c., would, at any rate at that time, be an obstacle to its reproduction.

H

Mr. Wright, of Paris, has kindly furnished some interesting notes, supplied by one who knew Watts Phillips well during the time he was residing in that capital.

"'Theodora' was brought out at the Surrey Theatre, April 9th, 1866, under the management of Mr. R. Shepherd; and the author, knowing what a cheese-paring kind of manager Dick Shepherd always was, added the following foot-note in the MS.:—'NOTE.—In the make-up of the coloured people in this drama, I pray the management to see that they are savage and *picturesque*, and not like *Ethiopian serenaders.*'

" He always asserted, and defied contradiction, that although living in France for years, he never produced a translation from the French but once, and that was his four-act drama of 'Not Guilty,' brought out at the Queen's Theatre, Long Acre, February 22nd, 1869, the principal parts being played by Messrs. Sam Emery, J. L. Toole, L. Brough, John Clayton, W. Stevens, Henry Irving, and Mrs. Labouchere (then Miss Henrietta Hodson).

" This piece was an adaptation of 'Le Comte de Sainte-Hélène,' a melodrama in five acts and seven *tableaux*, by MM. Desnoyer and Nus, and

A Quiet Family Disturbed

"Mutter!!! Why here are a dozen more coming"

"Why here are a Breechloaders down from London"

Dear M'. Milbank

Thanks for your very kind remembrance If as the poet says "beauty draws us by a single hair " M'. Phillips de.

"One for London! No return! Whenever Milbank comes down, I go up. there's no help for it"

GREAT NORTHERN RAILWAY.

LONDON

TICKETS

MARKET

acted for the first time at the Théâtre de la Gaîté, Paris, March 24th, 1849.

" At the time Watts Phillips lived in Paris, Benjamin Webster made it his study to pass most of his holidays there, so that he and Watts were almost inseparables ; they dined every Saturday and Sunday evening at the Hôtel Byron, Rue Favart, near the Opéra Comique. The hotel was supposed to be an English one, and was piloted by Jemmy Outhwaite, a stage gasfitter by trade, and who, during his career, had been employed at both the Adelphi and Lyceum theatres.

" He used to give a good English dinner for three francs, which sum included a half bottle of red or white wine.

" Phillips was a great friend and adviser of Mdme. Duverger, an actress noted more for her jewellery than stage talent. She was one night at the *Bal des Artistes*, then held annually at the Opéra Comique. She had on her neck one of the most handsome and valuable pearl three-rowed necklaces ever seen or worn even by royalty, which she was very near losing in consequence of the snap, through constant usage, giving way, so, for fear of them dropping, she

H 2

took them off her neck and carried them for a time in her hand.

"Whilst walking in the *foyer*, about three in the morning, her eyes by chance fell on Watts Phillips. Showing him what she held in her hand, and explaining that they might have been trampled on or lost, she gave them to him to guard until some time the next day.

"Watts had no sooner been put in possession of the necklace, than he walked to the mantel-piece, and took from his pocket a white handkerchief. Whilst in the act of carefully folding up the pearls, he was pounced on by two detectives, who were on duty and most gentlemanly made up in evening dress, and who there and then arrested him as an English 'swell mobsman.'

"Watts, who was a thorough French scholar, explained the situation of his being in possession of the necklace; but the officers and the mob by whom Watts was surrounded would not believe him, so that he was hustled out of the theatre and hurried off to the police station, in the Rue de Choiseul, where he was kept until eleven o'clock in the morning, it having unfortunately happened that when Mdme. Duverger left the theatre she did not go home, but went with a friend to supper and stayed in her company at her house until ten in the morning. When she reached her own dwelling she was met by a police agent, who, after explaining his errand, was sent off; but before he arrived at the station-house, Mdme. Duverger had been there and got poor Phillips liberated."

CHAPTER VII.

RETIREMENT TO EDENBRIDGE.

IN this year he was enabled, after a long absence, to return to England, where he was destined to reside for the rest of his life. It must have been a wrench for him to quit his much-loved Boulevards, where he had found so many friends. We have seen where his preference lay, and what a high opinion he held of the French nation.

The occasion of his return was the production of his new drama, "The Huguenot Captain," * of which piece he had great hopes. To add to its attraction he had brought from Paris some grotesque dancers, "The Clodoches," whose fantastic *pirouettes* caused astonishment. He established himself on Haverstock Hill, at Eaton Villas, where all his old friends—Webster, Toole, Clarke, Bel-

---

* This piece had a narrow escape from destruction. Mr. Coleman relates how it had been entrusted to him to bring to London, and how, in the hurry of the journey, he had lost it. After much trouble it was discovered at the Charing Cross Hotel, where it had been forgotten.

more, Mrs. Stirling, and others—gathered round
him. In Paris he had met and known that
attractive actress, Miss Neilson, who was now to
take the leading character in his play. There was
also that admirable *comédienne*, Mrs. Stirling, with
Augusta Thompson, and the showy, effective
Vining.

The cast was as follows:—

Characters.

Hector de Savigny (*Duc d'Armonville*).		Mr. J. Shore.
René de Pardillau { (*the Huguenot captain*) }		Mr. Vining.
Ambrose Paré .	. . .	Mr. W. R. Robins.
Annibal Locust .	. . .	Mr. George Honey.
Mousqueton .	. . .	Mr. R. Cathcart.
Etc.	Etc.	
The Duchess Jeanne .	. .	Mrs. Stirling.
Gabrielle	.	Miss Neilson.
Juanita .	. . . .	Miss Augusta Thompson.

The Ballet under the direction of Mr. Milano.

At last the long-delayed and much-buffeted
" Lost in London" was to be brought forward, a
piece with which its author always associated ill-
luck. Webster had intended performing the leading character, "Job Armroyd," himself, but was

obliged to withdraw, owing to illness.* The play was received with much applause, but the author's presentiments as to its being "unlucky" were to be justified.

Five years ago [he writes] I wrote the drama in question, with an eye to Mr. Benjamin Webster in the principal *rôle*, and it was to that gentleman I sold the London copyright. Since then the piece has been frequently in rehearsal, and a portion of the scenery painted, though circumstances over which I had no control postponed its production. Some time back Mr. Webster informed me that a person in his employ had *levanted* to America,

---

* In the bill was this rather unusual announcement:—" Mr. Benjamin Webster, finding recovery from his present serious illness to be impossible without perfect rest and relief from professional anxieties, has yielded to the advice of his medical adviser, Edwin Canton, Esq., and his friends, and prevailed upon Mr. Henry Neville to undertake the character originally written for Mr. Webster."

The caste of the play was as follows :—

Gilbert Featherstone { *(owner of the Blackmoor mine)* } . Mr. Ashley.

Job Armroyd (*miner*) . . . . Mr. H. Neville
(*his first appearance*).

Jack Longbones (*miner*). . . . Mr. Paul Bedford.

Benjamin Blinker (*a London tiger*). . Mr. J. L. Toole.

Tops (*a postboy*) . . . . . Mr. C. J. Smith.

Nelly . . . . Miss Neilson.

Tiddy Dragglethorpe . . . Mrs. Alfred Mellon
(*late Miss Woolgar*).

taking with him, besides other property, a MS. copy of
" Lost in London." The result of this act of rascality was
soon apparent, in the production, under another title, of my
unpublished, and hitherto unacted, piece at one or more of
the American theatres. Mr. Wallack, it appears, has now
gone to work with even greater boldness, restoring to the
stolen goods the original title. The drama of " Lost in
London " is entirely original.

I am perfectly well aware there is no law to protect a
published work or an acted drama from American piracy ;
*but this piece has neither been published nor acted—simply
stolen,* as much so as if my desk had been broken open, or
my watch drawn from my pocket.

The London copyright of " Lost in London " (a title, unfortunately, but too appropriate) belongs, as before said, to
Mr. Webster, and to that gentleman I refer for the truth of
the statements contained in this letter.

Notwithstanding ominous signs of rapidly failing health, the flow of new plays continued with
extraordinary abundance. In 1867 we hear of two
fresh pieces, "Nobody's Child," produced by Messrs.
Shepherd and Creswick, on September 14th, and
of "Maud's Peril," at the Adelphi, on October
23rd, in which that sympathetic actress, Miss
Herbert, had a part. Two other pieces were in
hand. "Fettered" was brought out at the Holborn
Theatre in February, 1869, and "Not Guilty" at
the Queen's in the same month. At the same time

two revived pieces of his, "Paper Wings" and "The Dead Heart" were being performed.

Thus was witnessed the almost unique spectacle of four plays from the same pen being in representation at the same moment. *

The agreeable, versatile author was now to find out that his own prolific gifts were an obstacle to the prosecution of his labours: while the eagerness of his many friends to enjoy his company, joined with his own relish for social delights, became a serious interruption. Not an hour could he call his own. Nor could this order of life be beneficial to his feeble health. Of a sudden he took the course of flying altogether from Town, and buried himself, at "The Firs," in the charming Kentish village of

* This phenonomen was thus commented upon in *Punch* :—

A THEATRICAL FOUR-IN-HAND.

Mr. Watts Phillips has performed—or shall we say, there has been performed by the aid of that gentleman—a theatrical feat which Mr. Punch holds it just to note. Four London theatres are now playing important pieces by Mr. Phillips, and three of these were produced within the same week. Of the respective and comparative merits of the leash, the Great Censor, having been too much engaged with Mr. Gladstone to have many spare evenings, does not as yet intend to say aught. But he has witnessed the revival of one of Mr. Phillips' plays, "The Dead Heart." He retains his opinion that this is one of the best Adelphi dramas which has ever been produced.

Edenbridge. This remedy was scarcely a wholesome one; and to a brilliant man of letters, who delighted in social converse, soon became intolerable. He fancied, however, that he found intense delight in this new rural attraction and in the company of his books.

> The country [he wrote] looks beautiful. Spring has come with a *burst*. What do you think of these two incidents? A stag leaped into our garden the other day, and we saw the full hunt come sweeping over hedge and ditch; then came the dogs after the stag, and we watched the chase for miles.
>
> The second incident took place half an hour ago, and the excitement continues. Sitting at my study window I saw a yard of snake crossing the road from the opposite field to our neighbour's front hedge, leaving its trail in the dust behind it. Everybody is out searching, but as yet, "no effects." Owing to the foolish destruction of the hedgehogs by the Farmers' Club last year, this part of Kent swarms with vipers, keeping up the garden of Eden analogy in admirable completeness. There is a great steeple-chase to-day within sight of the house.

He had now found many new friends, among whom was Mr.—now Sir Frederick—Milbank, who took a real interest in him, and Dr. Ord, the well-known physician. No one more cordially appreciated his versatile gifts. By Dr. Ord's valuable professional advice, and thoughtful kindness, he

was brought through many a serious crisis. To
both he addressed many of those gay, unre-
strained letters, so quaintly illustrated with some
of his most finished and humorous sketches,
which are such an adornment to this volume.
This has always seemed a most delightful exercise
of talent. The writer's fancy indulges itself in
irrepressible fancies, and the pen lends itself, as it
were, to these "gambols" without a thought of
"publication"; while there is evidence of a
geniality and goodwill in the devoting of time
and labour to the entertainment of friends.*

He wrote on January 1st, 1870—

I have received a most warm and long letter from Mr.
Milbank, a real friend to me. How much I appreciate his
friendship I need not say. He is still at Braham Castle,
but comes up for the opening of Parliament, and has given
me an invitation to his new town house in Cromwell
Gardens. [And later on] The other letter was from Mr.
Milbank, enclosing one from Mr. Algernon West (Gladstone's private secretary). It appears that a letter I wrote
to Mr. Milbank, with a drawing, has found its way into
the hands of the great "Don" himself. My opinions upon
the difficulties of the then present political situation of
parties was fully expressed.

---

* Sir Frederick Milbank and Dr. Ord have carefully preserved
a number of these fanciful efforts, which they have, in the kindest
way, placed at Miss Phillips' disposal.

Swanage

Portraits taken in this "Stile" Gratis

Respectfully dedicated to Mrs Ord

a student of many styles.

Mr. Milbank has asked me up to all the big political speeches, but I haven't been to *one* of them. I haven't even visited Cromwell Gardens since I last saw you. I get down among my books and let the world slide, the end of which will be, that if I go on as I am now doing, I shall slide very soon into my grave. Labouchere on his return from Paris gave a magnificent supper at the Queen's Theatre, to two hundred. I was the first consulted and asked, but I did not go. Nothing would suit me so well as an active political life; I'd rather talk than write, and one of these days I shall take Mrs. Chick's advice, and " make an effort."

P.S.—I have a cook on trial, who declares she has been cook at Baron Bramwell's, whose name thrusts itself into her conversation as the head of Charles I. did into Mr. Dick's memorial. Wonderful people have answered my advertisements in the country papers. One asked if followers were supplied. Another asks to sleep out three times a week, as her health requires it. A third wants a latch-key and the use of the piano when disengaged. A fourth refused to cook a hot dinner on a Sunday, "as displeasing to the Creator!"

Oh! what an ass they make of you!

I'm sick of servants! but then I'm sick of everything but sunshine, and am aweary and aweary with the paths of life. Like Lord Randal, I'm " sick at heart, and would fain lie down."

The house is looking perfectly charming; the beauty of the surrounding scenery is a compensation for many worries. I have an uninterrupted view for miles and miles around of meadow and upland; but the being here is a mistake. This is vegetating amidst vegetation. I avoid

society, and read tremendously. Get up at four in the
morning and read Political Economy, Ruskin, and John
Mill.

I have never been in front of a curtain at the theatre
since I left London, and when I do go up it is from invita-
tions from managers. I had a ticket sent me for the
Theatrical Fund Dinner, with an invitation to speak.

Your questions about "Axe and Crown" (it's like the
sign of a public-house) I can't answer, not having seen
it.*

What a difference between this and Hill's Place, where
I had too many friends swarming in at all hours, and now
Zimmermann himself could not live in a more complete
solitude.

I see this *on dit* in all the papers: "Mr. Watts
Phillips is busily employed in writing a comedy of modern
life, as well as a new drama." Who has spread it, I don't
know. I certainly have the pieces on the stocks, but the
stocks are one thing and the funds another.

At this time the French and German war had
broken out, and, from his ardent sympathies with
the *grande nation*, he felt in the most poignant
way the sufferings that were overwhelming it. As
he said, "I can't write about it. I feel my heart
lacerated with indignation." In many little touching ways he shows his feeling, as when he thought

---

* The late Mr. John Forster used to be equally merry on this
odd title, protesting that it could only be pronounced "Twix' Tax
and Crown."

of the poor honest innkeepers with whom he used to stay at St. Lieu. " I read a few days ago that the Prussians would soon be in St. Lieu. I now see that the Chassins are utterly, hopelessly ruined; their vineyards are destroyed, their inn abandoned, their farm produce seized, and the whole family, who had lived at St. Lieu for centuries, fugitives in Paris. The news brought honest tears into my eyes as I read."

He was more distressed when he learned of the crowds of ruined refugees taking refuge in London, and had recourse to an odd device to save himself from the pain of refusing an assistance which he could not afford. He wrote to his friend Coleman:—

Will you favour me by posting in Glasgow the enclosed, and should any letters be sent to me under "your care," please post them back here. The key to the mystery is this :—Crowds of friends whom I knew in Paris in better times are *swarming* over to London, especially French actors and actresses, whom I should only be too happy to serve *were it in my power*, but, alas ! I can't *procure* them what I *want* so badly for myself. Nor, busy as I am, can I afford the time to hasten, at every letter, up to London and listen to their miseries, a *sad* task at any time, doubly so when what they expect is impossible ! So, to have a quiet Christmas, I have said that I have taken a few days' holiday to visit you in Scotland.

To the same trusted friend he sent this characteristic *épanchement* :—

Wish I could get away, but this war keeps me as closely tied to the desk as a galley-slave is to his bench. My *long, long* acquaintance with France and things French has made my pen of late in constant requisition; but, oh! what a sad business it is! My heart bleeds while I write. Whatever France's faults were, she deserves every brave and honest man's sympathy now. Let us cut ourselves away from the dead corpse of the *Past ;* it is with the heroic *Present* we have to do. *I* love France as much as I despise those smug and self-sufficient traitors who have brought her to this pass; as much as I hate the moral ugliness of that "pseudo Privy Councillor of God," Holy King William, who stalks over a battle-field on Bible stilts, and thanks Providence at each new act of murder.

Ah, old boy, if you had only known France as I have known her—not the putrescent society of Paris, which, like fish in the dirt, glittered from its rottenness, but the France of the workshop and the field, the France that is now fighting while its demoralised army is in captivity, and that will fight on to the bitter end—you'd be as sad as I am at the bloody work that is going on.

There is one thing, be assured, this war will do, viz., sweep away the lardy-dardy, frivolous puff pastry which has so long defiled our stage. The age of confectionery is at its death-grips. After every great national convulsion in France there has been a *change* in England. There will be a *great one* now. When a nation has passed through the valley of the shadow, it begins to *think.*

"My dear Tartar
'What are the red
coals saying?'"

Cats?

thine DW

Very Unhappy!

"What are the red coals saying? Why
that they've gone up 2/. a ton said
that makes me very unhappy!'"

France is passing through a Red Sea and will come out purified.

England's time of trial is not far off. In politics, in war, in literature, *men* will come to the front. Phryne, with her leer and her breakdown, Sporus, with his drawl and his simper, will pass away from us, as they have vanished for years to come from France. Our authors must do something more than cater for the jaded appetites of the swell and his "lady," the inanity of the drawing-room and the vice of the boudoir. Above all, the public will demand other actors than those who treat all dramatic creations as the Italian image man treats the casts he carries on his head, polishing down every salient feature, till Shakespeare might pass for the Marquis of Lorne, and Milton and Molière for B—— and P——.—With a warm shake of the hand, yours sincerely.

He was busy, as usual, with a number of dramas. For his favourite piece "Marlborough" he was still struggling to secure a hearing, but with little success. All the persons to whom it was offered spoke of it with the "highest respect," and even admiration, but somehow were "shy" of taking it in hand. It was shaped and re-shaped to their taste, but without result. One manager, Mr. Vining, oddly enough, bought only the *last* act; but later secured the previous ones. It was finally made a present of to Mr. Coleman, who still holds it. Our author had also in hand "Trial

I

by Jury," with other pieces. At this time it began to dawn upon him that his system of wholesale manipulation might not be so profitable as the more careful and deliberate one of concentrating his whole energies on single efforts to be produced at long intervals. This was a wholesome view, but such discoveries often come too late, when the powers have been dissipated and the old habit is too strong. He proclaims his new view to his friend Coleman in a most characteristic epistle.

EAGLE LODGE,

EDENBRIDGE, KENT,

April 18*th*, 1870.

MY DEAR COLEMAN,—First of all a warm and friendly shake of the hand, then to plunge into the "middle of things" and talk of business. Twelve months ago, I had two pieces produced in London, both without the success very many previous productions of mine have received. Here are the facts.

Labouchere brought me a French piece (a bad one) with a *big sensation scene.* "Will you adapt this piece for me?" he inquired. I replied that I didn't see a success, and was answered that he was prepared to pay a big price, and that if I did not do it Tom Taylor would jump at it, and that Halliday would do it at one-third what either of us would charge. I adapted the piece, pouched a good sum, and the result was what I had predicted.

Another manager had a mania that "low life sensation" was the one thing needed to make a theatre. What Tommy Dod had done for one piece a "rat-pit" would do for another. Again I gave way, and this time the failure was positive. I pocketed the coin, read the criticisms, and made a resolve never to write another piece unless I had some belief in the subject, and some higher aim than the mere £ s. d.

Acting upon this resolve, and pretty confident as to the fate of most of the stuff so rapidly turned out of the theatrical oven, I have withdrawn for a time from the arena, nursing whatever little talent I have, to keep it warm, but (and I say it most sincerely) disdaining the "you scratch me and I'll scratch you" mode of doing business, which fills the *press* with eulogies of "certain dramatists," and empties the *theatres!* I don't want to write again for the stage till I have the opportunity of creating an *honestly* strong comedy or drama in which there is something else to be worked for besides the (always welcome) £ s. d.

So, like our ancient Roman friend, I retire among my cabbages, and get my bread and cheese, with now and then a glass of claret, by writing novels and "articles for that Palladium of British liberty, the immaculate and never (oh, never!) prejudiced press.

Show me a really good subject for a strong, healthy drama, and I will pounce upon it with avidity, but don't let either of us be misled because certain celebrities are "popular."

I was asked to adapt *Frou-Frou.* I refused the money because I believed F.-F. was *rot*, and would never draw a sensible British audience. It was only popular in France because it tickled the outer cuticle of immorality.

I 2

Not so *Patrie*—a very noble drama, though *revolting* (like some of the plays of that mighty genius Hugo), but a *great drama* for all that, though an impossible one for England, where Sodom dreads no other fires than those Captain Shaw and his brigade can efficiently deal with ; where all is allowed if the curtain be down, and where vice is virtue if it be well concealed.

We have heaps of clever dramatists in brain and heart, but banality rules the *hour.* Your friend Charles Reade (with whom I see you are staying) is a noble exception. *He* never writes without *thinking*, and even his *worst* books are redolent of genuine endeavour of the best kind, and full of *manly* strength and tenderness.

It's not for me to advise in business matters, my dear Coleman, or to speculate in London. Your material *must* be pure metal, and pure metal is not to be obtained without many a painful process.

What I should want to write a piece such as I wish to write, and would try to write for you, would be a fair sum paid (pardon my being frank in business matters) a portion down, to enable me to cast aside *other work* for the time being, and the remainder as we may, after consultation, determine.

Everything in London is in a deplorable state. *No* theatre is really making money at the present time. What may be done is yet to be seen.

In May he wrote—

I write in haste, as you may imagine when I tell you that I am under strict bond to write in six weeks from May 1st a comedy, of which I have only as yet produced the skeleton idea. I went up on Friday last to sign the

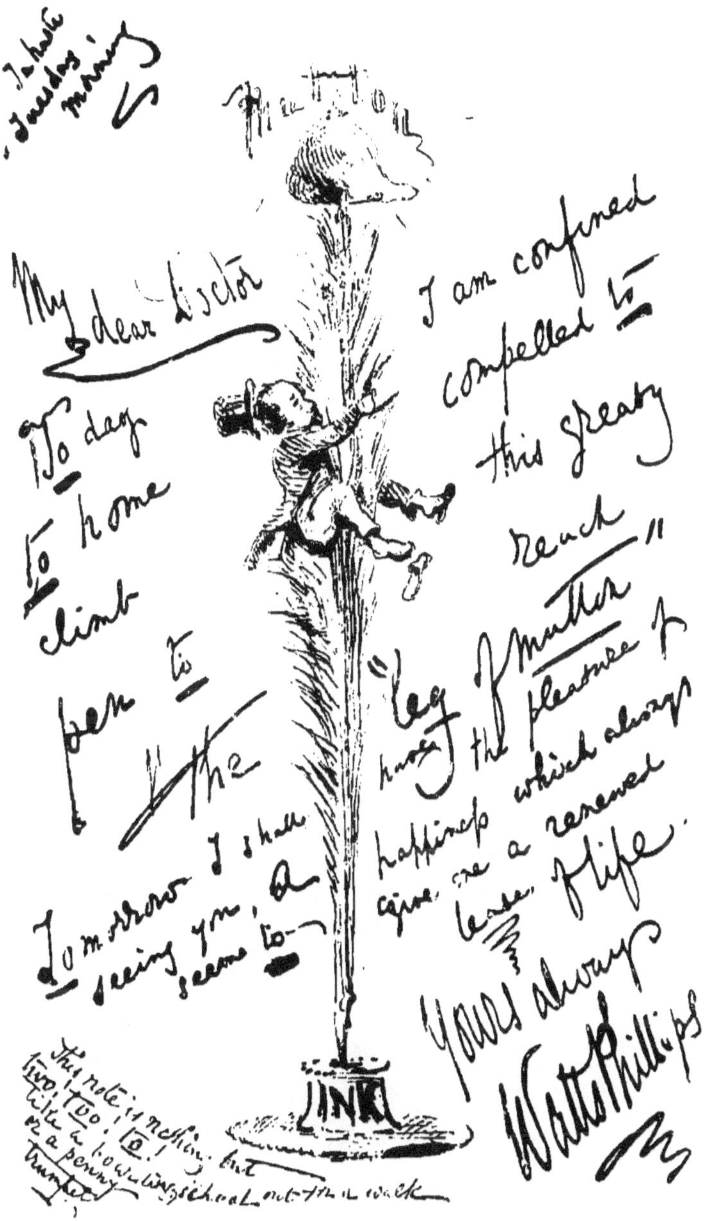

agreement. I had promised myself to come and see you, but, being in town so seldom, I was overwhelmed with business with Phelps, Beverley, and others, breaking, perforce, several appointments. Then I had to dine with Labouchere at the Reform, and in the evening be at Mrs. Crabbe's (Miss Herbert). The next day I lunched with Mr. Milbank. I dined with Webster and Chatterton (fancy my miserable digestion!) and had to rush to catch the last train at 8.50.

The country here is simply fairy-land—beautiful—but I *must* come nearer London. I am bullied on every side, and in last week's *Day's Doings* appeared an article (I am totally ignorant by whom) upon the state of the drama, and asking "What has become of Watts Phillips?" Very complimentary, saying that my fault was "writing too well."

CHAPTER VIII.

RETURN TO TOWN—FAILING HEALTH AND DEATH.

ABOUT this time he found that living at the romantic Edenbridge, however great its pastoral charm, kept him too far from the sphere of his professional labours. He now fixed himself in town at No. 45, Redcliffe Road,* and was presently very busy superintending the rehearsals of " On the Jury."

* From his new house he sent out a pleasant little handbill, which notified to his friends his change of quarters—

WATTS PHILLIPS,

45, REDCLIFFE ROAD, REDCLIFFE GARDENS,
SOUTH KENSINGTON.

W P. respectfully informs the Nobility, Gentry, and his Friends in general, that he has commenced Business at the above address.

Orders will be executed with punctuality, cleanliness, and dispatch.

𝔖𝔥𝔢𝔯𝔯𝔶 𝔞𝔫𝔡 𝔆𝔦𝔤𝔞𝔯𝔰 𝔴𝔥𝔢𝔫 𝔠𝔞𝔩𝔩𝔢𝔡 𝔣𝔬𝔯.

W. P. has also a spirit licence, but no one will be allowed to get drunk on the premises.

N.B.—It is requested that this notice will be hung in a prominent part of the kitchen.

The piece [we find him writing February, 187-] has been a big success, and, but for Phelps, would be carried on (it is just possible) beyond Easter. He makes arrangements, however, for Manchester, Birmingham, Liverpool, and Dublin after that date, to take the comedy with him, but Chatterton (Phelps' engagement, a long one, expiring at Easter) will not renew it in London for the terms he asks—£60 per week—the sum he is now receiving. It is preposterous, but there is no reasoning with him, and when Heaven calls to Samuel it must be in the silvery or golden accents of £ s. d. The comedy will appear in New York, Philadelphia, New Orleans, *Chicago!!!!* What a people !! [This was after the fire of Chicago, which had just been rebuilt.] Boston and San Francisco within the next four months. The Duke of Edinburgh, with my dear old young friend Eliot Yorke (the Earl of Hardwicke's son) came round to compliment Phelps and Webster ; Eliot regretting that " dear old Watts " was not there. All speaks well for the piece. I had a pleasant hour on Saturday, for going to the Princess' on business (I *never* go, if I can help it, after the first night to see a piece of my own. The faults are too glaring, and you are ready to cut your throat to think how much *better* you *ought* to have done it), I met Theodore Martin (Bon Gaultier) and his accomplished wife (ex-Miss Helen Faucit), Bellew, and a heap of people. All more than warm as regards the play; all thinking the " sensation " scene might have been left out. I told them that to introduce it (it was introduced after the piece was written) I was compelled to twist a three-act comedy into a four-act drama, and clip out strong writing for the scene painter; but Chatterton swore by the "*gods,*" and I fancy he was, in the £ s. d. view, right.

I am not at all well. Like Sterne's starling, "I can't get out," which, for a walker like myself, a lover of long rambles in town or country, is death. But I have signed articles to have an original piece ready, "Black Mail," for the Adelphi by Easter. Impossible. I don't adapt; I don't translate; and they will have to wait. Nevertheless, they worry me dreadfully. Say I'm "the man risen up from the dead, and must work double time till I go into the country and *sleep again.*" All very *well*, but I'm very *ill*, for all that, and should cave in but for congenial companionship.

You will not see "Marlborough" this spring; there is a slight row about it. I'm wanted to design scenes, dresses, etc. I require £50 if I suggest dresses, draw them, and scenes, as I am now doing for the Adelphi. Vining agreed to everything. A great earthquake took place. Liston is to go out of the theatre; Vining will, possibly, still hold on. W. P——— having nothing to gain by "Marlborough" but fame, and caring very little about squeezing such a piece into such a tiny, tin-pot theatre, sits like a painted angel on a cloud, grinning at the strife. It is a sort of free fight; but *I* stand out. Altogether G. V. has paid about £450 for "Marlborough." Well, I hope he'll get the money back; but he must be quick. It appears that Sothern (who first purchased the play) sent a copy to America, and before long it is possible, I hear, that it will be done in splendid style over there. Vining swears by the piece as "the biggest I have ever, etc., etc., etc."

On Friday, Sala, Labouchere, myself, and some others went over Newgate by special invitation from Sheriff Bennet and the Under-Sheriff, given to me, and I asked the party. We shall have lots to talk about when we meet.

We were two hours and a half going over, and Labouchere has described the visit in the same amount of columns in the *Daily News.*

Can't write any more. Miss Furtado is coming here about some songs which I am introducing into her part, and I must go and comb my scanty remnant of hair. I'll send Harrison a box; he's a good fellow—a very good fellow.

Now, good-bye! my hair is still uncombed and Furtado approaches.—Yours,   WATTS.

Labouchere and I supped with the Claimant last week. Think it possible I dine at L.'s with Ballantine, Spofforth, and Sir Roger Orton Tichborne next Sunday. Will tell you all about it when we meet.

*   *   *   *

I am ill, angry, put out *every way.*

"Marlborough" comes out at Brighton on the 21st. I have neither time nor inclination to go down to see it.

A few days ago I got a notice from the Queen's Theatre that Sir Charles Young's play had proved worse than a failure, a "Calamity," and that they had put "Amos Clark"* in *immediate* rehearsal. I wrote and *protested.* No good! Labouchere is on the Continent. A "scratch" company. So, like Achilles, I remain in my tent—very grand, but d——d uncomfortable. Oxenford and Charles Reade dined with me, or rather, I dined with *them,* the other day. The one was full of "Amos" which he had read, and the other of "Marlborough," which Vining had (without my knowledge) given Charles to "Reade." Rignold is Amos.

Well, never mind, Achilles will not quit his tent, but

---

* Dramatised from his novel of that name.

glowers and meditates taking the altitude of a bridge. "Amos Clark" is half reconstructed. I want to get a copy of "Amos" to America by next mail, in a forlorn hope of getting it out before the Yankee thieves can obtain any shorthand copies. The Queen's people think "Amos" will be a great go.

No! No! No! With Wigan or Hermann Vezin, yes; possibly a big Yes!

I haven't finished the Princess' piece yet, though it is approaching its termination. It's a peculiar production at least.

I'm in disgrace *everywhere.* Nobody loves me. Vining is pelting me with letters from Brighton, and the knocker is nearly wrenched off my door by messengers from the "Queen's," but poor, grumpy Achilles still sulks in his tent and doesn't show. The game is not worth the candle.— Thine, WATTS.

At Redcliffe Road he saw much of his agreeable neighbour—the ever-vivacious Sala—perhaps the most original writer of our day. From him came many a pleasant reminder of his vicinity—such as a visiting card, with this humorous epigraph :—

> *I have been choking the whole week, and never out of my room. Convalescent for a little. Come in to-morrow evening. Quite alone. You shall hear my new cough. Come! Do!*
>
> ### Mr. George Augustus Sala,
> ### Reform Club.
>
> *Correspondant du Journal,*
> *Le "Daily Telegraph,"*
> *Londres,*
> *et ami de l'humanité.*

My love to Mrs. Old !

Boo—oo

The only malady the doctor
cannot cure

a mere sketches
and have
only

enough strength left to sign myself
Very truly yours
Watts Phillips

Friday Morning—in Bed—

A little better, but still d——d bad

DEAR WATTS,—Can you lend me a copy of "Elia," the "Old Benchers of the Temple," for half an hour? I think I am up to writing a leader to-day about a point in connection therewith.

If you are well enough, come and see a cove *to-day after four.* Doctors come at half-past three. G. A. S.

Unhappily this topic of ill-health was one on which both might claim reciprocal sympathy. How acutely the overworked dramatist was suffering at this time will be seen from the following letter to his physician, Dr. Canton.

I am much better; your prescription has relieved my pain greatly, but it *returns* at the least excitement, but not with the same cruel intensity as before. I stick manfully to my work, as I am in honour bound to do; but when you see friends Chatterton and Churchill, oblige me by saying how ill I have been—how ill I *am.* I should not like them to think me idle (idle!!! ye gods! and working on in the pain I am suffering), nor careless of my promise. Do this for me and oblige your friend and debtor, WATTS.

"Amos Clarke," a pleasing, emotional drama, was now brought out and introduced by that capable actress Miss Wallis to the London stage. It was well received, and is likely to be revived. The author was called for, and now, I believe for the first time, yielded to the favourite custom of being "called before the curtain." As he bowed his acknowledgments, he did not perhaps think that this was to be the last of his long series of pieces that would be presented to an audience. In his storehouse, however, he had still others waiting performance, such as "Black Mail," "A Rolling Stone," and "Doctor Cape- dose's Pill." But his illness was fast gaining on him, enfeebling all his energies, as will be seen from his last pathetic letters. These shall speak for him as the others have done hitherto.

It has got about that I am ill—I am rarely seen in public, and birds of ill-omen—bless their cruel beaks!— shake their heads. I dare not go abroad in *that* weather. I have firm faith in Dr. Ord, but we are apt to get impatient when the recovery is a slow one. Luckily the brain was never better.

Here's another bit of my luck. The great Edwin Booth took my "Marlborough" and "Amos" to bring out at his theatre. I refused a dozen other offers—left everything to him. He has suddenly been declared a bankrupt, and the theatre—best in New York—has gone smash, and there's an end for me for a time.

The enclosed—which please return—tells the true story of "Black Mail." My luck again! Chatterton was mad about the piece, and thought of Emery and George Honey (if they could not get the American genius J. C. Clarke) for the part. Chatterton comes back to the Adelphi, but Webster will not have "B. M" done without him, and that cannot be. But never despond. Remember what poor dear Tom Hood said, " If your heart is hung too low, the more reason to keep it up."

Thank God for books !—I can bear illness—I can bear almost anything—if I can bury my nose in the pages of a book, while I never forget

> " Each inly 'plains, and, in his weariness,
> Envies his neighbour, racked by like distress.
> None estimates the pains that others feel,
> Since, as he hides his own, they theirs conceal ;
> He bends his head, and murmurs in his heart,
> ' The world is *blessed,* I only stand apart.' "

André Chenier said this, but, after all, he was guillotined. Like André Chenier, I suppose I too shall die with a brag (at least it will be an honest one) and tapping my marble forehead assert " that there *was* something there."

Here's an egotistical letter for you !—I'm ashamed of it, so farewell.   WATTS.

Tichborne called upon me last night, very smart and clean, but there's a decided touch of Wapping.

And again—

The barometer of my health marks changeable. I lie awake o' nights, and like Mr. Eugene Aram, I "stare aghast at sleep." Dr. Ord says that I must have patience ; (patience ! ! ! ye gods !)—that I am going on well, and that he is sure to pull me through. I shall never be the Sampson, to say nothing of the Adonis, I once was. At present he might " pull me through " the eye of a needle. You might photograph me as Milton's " Death," " a shadow of a shadow." I have commenced my new story, but as yet, progress but slowly. Chatterton has not been up to dinner, but is " coming." In fact, there is no theatre at his command for " Black Mail." When he ordered it he had the Princess', and the Adelphi, and mine was to have been a continued engagement—but in a week, the whole bright edifice crumbled in. No small theatre will reimburse Chatterton's outlay for " Black Mail," and so time goes on, and what was fresh becomes antiquated.

Last Sunday I was knocked up. That noble fellow, Ord—it being his only day—came up in his carriage to see how I was. With him came Mrs. Ord. In the evening entered Labouchere, then Sala and Mrs. Sala. Oh, horror ! The Duke of Clarence never passed a worse night than I did, and I had *no* Malmsey in the morning.

Labouchere has bought Pope's villa at Twickenham.

No. You have mistaken a little about " Black Mail." I wanted to know your ideas, whether the advent of Kenyon at the conclusion of the piece, as Duke of Atherston would be understood by that most exacting of playgoers, the " Pot-boy in the gallery." But we'll have a long chat soon—a long, or rather to myself, a *short* day—and huddled together round a handful of coal (bring us a lump in your muff), talk pleasantly of everything and everybody.

How I pray for quiet ! I ought to live twenty years longer, and do something more, and something better. I am very patient, and few see under the mask I wear ; but it will be hard indeed if, after my long illness, and patient obedience to the Doctor, I am to be printed in sheets, bound in boards, issued by the Brompton Cemetery, and republished—God knows *where.* I have sent the " Rolling Stone " to Neville. It makes me *mad* sometimes that I cannot go myself, but, Ord says, any sudden movement on my part may throw me back, and when I ask the managers to come to me, they don't leave till they hear the chimes at midnight.

What a changed man I am! A year's self-communing makes even a *fool* think. I am not near, near, near well. Never shall be! I only pray to keep my *head* above the rising water, and that the Lord will "keep my memory green."

Good-bye! God bless you all in the "ring fence of home," and let us hope that what seems a superstition may prove a truth, and we all have happier lives hereafter.

I know your friend Robert Brome very well; he was a fourth-rate poet, and for some time a servant to Ben Jonson, wielding a *broom* in right good earnest. Ben says

> "I had you for a servant once, Dick Brome,
> And you perform'd a servant's faithful parts ;
> Now you are got into a nearer room,
> Of fellowship," etc. etc.

And the brave old boy backed his servant to the last !

WATTS.

At this season of distress, when the end was not far away, reappears his old master pictorial in art, the veteran George Cruikshank, whose friendly visits must have comforted him.

DEAR FRIEND AND PUPIL [wrote the veteran on *December 3rd*, 1872],—It so happens that I am engaged every evening this week, and so return the tickets—but shall be glad to

have one for next week, and will arrange for the day, or
rather the evening.

I have been wanting to see you for a long time, and
made *two* attempts to discover " Redcliffe Road," but was
lost in the wilderness of the *Bromptons;* so, presuming that
the lessons I gave you in the " art of drawing" will enable
you to sketch out a map of that part of the globe, I shall
be obliged if you will favour me with such a sketch, and I
will announce, with a *flourish of the pen,* when I propose to
give you a call, so that you may be prepared to meet your
old Friend and Master.—Yours truly, GEORGE CRUIKSHANK.

December 14th, 1872.

DEAR WATTS PHILLIPS,—The weather has been very
severe in these northern parts, quite " Ice-bound," and then
such a thaw—that I was afraid of being " Water-logged,"
but as there now seems to be a favourable change, I am
preparing for my journey to the south-west, and hope to
arrive at the " Red Cliffs " on next Monday afternoon, about
5 o'clock P.M.*—and trust to find you all—all well.   There
are two routes I find to your part of the world ; one " *over*-
land," and the other " *under*-land," and I shall travel by
the latter to the place you name—and then, with your excellent map in hand, plunge into the wilderness, feeling
sure that I shall be sure to find " Wigwam " forty-five.

My wife and I went to see " Amos Clarke," and were
delighted to make his acquaintance ; more of this anon.
But now one word further—if Monday is not convenient to
you, telegraph by cable, or any other way you're able, to
yours truly,   GEORGE CRUIKSHANK.

* Being a " T.T.," I name this hour as it is about my *T.*-time.

Later the old artist wrote—

And now I must tell you that ever since I saw that play of " Lost in London " I have been "going to write" and "going to call" to tell you that, although I must confess that I *did* like to see the *play*, I did *not* like the audience to *see* me *a-crying* like a *baby*—however, more of this anon. All I shall add now is, that of course you will take it for *granted.* that I thank you for the letter to Grant. And as I intend to return to town on Wednesday, 6th, you will, if you please, expect me to name an early evening, at an early hour, on an early day, to receive the muffins, crumpets, etc. etc. etc."

A sort of weary despondency will be noticed in the last few letters of our dramatist.

February 28th, 1873.

I have been very ill and in great pain, weak and nervous to that degree that the slamming of a door, or partially raised voice, produced both bodily and mental suffering. I do not sleep at nights; however, " it is an ill wind," etc., for I prop myself up in bed and write, *slap through the night,* " copy," wild and weird, restless as life and sad as death. Night writing *is* death ; but what a delicious time it is ! The whole discord of the day shut out. The horrible *row of living* forgotten in the *exquisite quiet,* unbroken but by the step of a passing policeman, or the squeak of a mouse (we have mice by the *hundred* here).

Night, midnight, to me a realisation of all that is tranquil and happy, and I am sorry when my solitary vigil is broken by the screech of the milkman.

I am much, oh ! so much better to-day, and fancy that

J

I may for a period have a good time of it; but who can
answer for to-morrow? A fit of passion, and a man topples
over with heart-disease. A week of bad weather, and down
goes the nervous man trembling with pain, or standing
wrestling with his agony, like Laocöon with his snakes.

Dr. Richardson called upon me the other day with
George [Cruikshank]. In the absence of Dr. Ord he would
not even feel my pulse. "I know Ord," he said, "a very
clever man;" and so, while he shook the hand, refused to
touch the wrist. He had, I imagine, a pleasant visit,
though I *forced* myself into form; and, if there was not
much wit, there was much laughter. Webster will gain
more than £2,000 by his benefit. I'm on the committee,
but never once been near.

So they've run the Claimant in at last; fourteen years
are pretty stiff, but after the lucid summing up none can
doubt that he is Arthur Orton. So I shall have much
gossip when we meet. Sala was here last night, having
seen the *last* of him—a most vivid description. The
brougham waiting for "orders" at one door of Westminster
Hall and "Black Maria" swallowing him up at another!
The Radcliffe business swamped him. Tichborne or Orton,
the gorge of the nation rose against him.

45, REDCLIFFE ROAD,
March 10*th*.

What do you think of Sir Roger Arthur Orton Castro
now? I am so glad I have seen and closely studied the
man; so closely that I can imitate to an accent and a
gesture. What a huge fraud! The great nineteenth
century phenomenon.

It is now five o'clock, Wednesday morning, and I am writing this in bed, unable to sleep. Mrs. Sala says Fleet Street is crowded, the issue of the *Daily Telegraph* being too slow for the *enormous* demand.

I hope we've heard nearly the last of the great Tichborne case, and that when " they've run in" Luie, the cook, shopman, and the " sly grog-shop keeper" we shall talk of something else. I was invited to a swell dinner, where upon every plate was a card, " *Le Tichborne est defendu,*" which reminds me with a shudder that I haven't slept a wink; but I have to go down to see Ord—he must be sick of me ; I am of myself—and have *to go out to dinner to-night at eight ! ! !* I cannot put it off; it's to meet Mr. Milbank, Osborn, etc. I have broken so many appointments that, if alive, I *must* go.

Would you like to see " Ought We to Visit Her" ? Labouchere tells me it is a success ; I enclose card, fill in date. George Crookedlegs (as such was his announcement to the servant) called a little time ago. What a wonderful old chap he is ! He sits drinking tea, and eating muffins, and joking by the hour. R. gave him "Dora," and he made a pretty speech, ending with, " You have made the old man, who has made so many laugh, cry, my dear." Good-bye, for it is now daylight, and my lamp looks as sickly as I do !—Yours,   WATTS.

I am glad to hear that " our cousin" (Mr. "John" Jellicoe) is making such rapid advance with his pencil. I knew he would. He is a clever young fellow.

In these troubled, closing days of his life he was much cheered and his sufferings alleviated by the

J 2

kindly solicitude of his friend and medical adviser, Dr. Ord. In the letters which he addressed to this gentleman are found touching expressions of gratitude for many services rendered, lightened by his usual vein of pleasantry. These letters, too, are enriched by pen-and-ink sketches of extraordinary merit and finish, full of fancy and lively humour. This finish and delicacy, which must have been the result of many hours' exertion, were expended for the entertainment of his friend, and meant, no doubt, as some feeble return for kindness which he could not otherwise acknowledge.

TO DR. ORD'S BULL-DOG "TARTAR." *

(With a print.)

MY DEAR TARTAR!

My cream of all the Tartars, and chief of all the Tartar 'Ords!

I am going to make you a little present. Our interviews have hitherto been but short ones, but I know you love me from the way you always investigate the calf of my leg to see if there is not *yet* some little meat there and how the bone is getting on.

With this letter you will receive your *portrait*, framed and glazed! You'll not be offended if I say you have an ugly mug, Tartar; but there are uglier mugs still manu-

---

* This letter was accompanied by a fine etching, by Lipic, after Jadin. It was the portrait of a bull-dog, "Jupiter."

factured in the Potteries, and many uglier dogs (though *they* don't think it) in the photographers' windows. Besides, with you, like with Mirabeau, another ugly dog, your ugliness covers a great soul.

Take my picture, Tartar, and show it to your good master and missis; they will appreciate it, for it is a fine etching—now *rare*—and full of power. Give my love to your young master and your young misses, and wish them a merry Christmas and the *happiest* of *happy New Years!*

Good-bye, old fellow! I was a jolly dog once, though somewhat of a sad one now; and if ever you see a stranger, with a particularly long mug, wandering Streatham way, look on his collar for the name of

WATTS PHILLIPS.

December 22nd, 1873.

To Dr. Ord.

July 16th, 1873.

Glad to hear you are so jolly—living in such a style (stile)-ish manner, and picking up those inconsiderable trifles which, passing through the alembic of your brain, become more than sterling gold. I think I see you in my "mind's eye, Horatio," striding along on those "splendacious" legs—Antinous, Apollo, Hercules, and Æsculapius rolled into one.

I thought of writing something about London, but—why poison your fresh and innocent mind; and blacken the sunshine you are revelling in with smoky jest and foggy stories from this great city?

As regards myself, I am *much* better. I enclose my bill of fare—I mean my bill of health—that you may judge of the progress I have made.

I hope you are bringing back lots of " wise simples "—
Sundew sounds nice. Do you think it would suit me with
ice and sugar—a solution of Bog-weed taken alternately as
a tonic ?

Good-bye ; if *brevity* is really the soul of *wit*, I congratulate you on this letter.

With kind regards,

Yours always sincerely,

WATTS PHILLIPS.

TO THE SAME.

How do you like Swanage ? I hear there is a very
pleasant cove named Punfold in the neighbourhood ; when
you see him greet him for me.   You will also come across
some nice fellows, friends of his, Firestone, Gault, Green-
sand, and Wealden.   These were their names when I knew
them, but, as their means have grown *strata* and *strata*,
it is possible they may have changed them.

Can't I see you at breakfast, revelling over the *broiled*
bone of an *Iguanodon*. I am informed that a crocodile
was found (1837) at Swanage—of course, in a fossil state ;
the pretty creature had wept itself to death, and, after
writing its will on a slab of calcareous slate, had died
upon a bed of " fawn-coloured " limestone with a sweet
smile on its mouth.

After all, there must have been great larks in those
pre-Adamite ages, and it must have been an improving
and touching sight to see the infant Saurians going to
school, with their little calcareous slates under their arms.

No more space ! or I had a lot more to say, as I think
I never write so well as upon subjects of which I am

profoundly _ignorant_. Of one thing, however, I am profoundly sensible, that I am always yours most sincerely,

WATTS PHILLIPS.

To Dr. Ord's Daughter Christine.

MY DEAR CHRISTINE,

I send this letter to you by a very old friend of mine, a _giant_, but such a good fellow that, though he loves you so much that he could _almost_ eat you up, he would not hurt a hair of your pretty head—no, not for a hundredweight of toffee or a ton of barley sugar. I knew him when I was a little boy, such a little boy that I always went in and out the keyhole without opening the door. If you can go through the keyhole, it is so much better, you know, because you never leave the door open, and dear papa and mama will never catch cold. The only danger is that you might catch the lock-jaw, and that would be a pity. I was looking over my library the other day, and found another book, the same I gave your big sisters, and I thought, Why should not —— have a set of giants and fairies _all to herself_—to look over them in her own pretty way, and to talk to them in her own sweet fashion? So, darling, I send you the book. Excuse my very short letter, but I am " greengaged " to a friend, and in a great hurry—but believe me, your affectionate friend and admirer,   WATTS PHILLIPS.*

---

* Addressed (writes Dr. Ord) to one of my daughters, then a very little girl. The book was "Grimm's Fairy Tales," illustrated by G. Cruikshank. The child told her mother to write and say that "the man who drawed those pictures was the best drawer that ever drawed." The letter arrived while Cruikshank

To Dr. Ord.

My dear Doctor,

The "winter of my discontent" has set in! The cabmen demand half the sum that would ransom the French to take me a dozen yards! The "busses" refuse to take me *at all.* Where am I living??? In Siberia? At Spitzbergen? We are *snowed in!* All of us are "bewhaling" our fate, and the knife-boy has taken to *blubber.* We have no coals in our cellar, but plenty of colds in our heads. Ugh! no more North-West Passages for me! No more writing up the Naval Phrenologists who are so anxious to finger the bumps of the Pole! My household wealth, however, has somewhat increased, for I have three *scrapers* at my door. For my own part, I am not at all well; with a spine like an icicle (my North Pole), and a brain like an iceberg, but a heart like Nebuchadnezzar's furnace, yours "warmly,"

WATTS PHILLIPS.

To the Same.

My dear Doctor,

As Professor Max Müller would say, I take it for *granted* you have returned to town. I have been called away to Birmingham, etc., to arrange about "Amos Clark," which Mr. Rignold is taking about the country. Each time I have taken up a pen to write to you, I have thrown

---

was breakfasting with Watts Phillips, and gave the old artist great pleasure. Phillips told me that he got up from table and danced round the room, saying that it was one of the finest compliments he had ever received.

it down, feeling the impossibility of my writing the letter I wished to write. It wanted to be brilliant, but the spirit of Dogberry was upon me, and I wrote myself . . you can fill in the rest. You know the definition of a pen, " a feather plucked from the pinion of a goose to write down the opinion of another." I dared not inflict my tediousness, my bitter complaints, my eternal melancholy. " Sir," says one of " Ben " Jonson's characters, addressing in the *polite* fashion of that time a casual friend, " you are out of sorts; you have your brains in your belly and your guts in your head." This is still my position, and I am under bond to write a new piece, to do more rash acts for the managers, and sit on the points of my own jokes ! I hope you've been jolly; in fact, I know you have been so, for you essentially possess " the harvest of a quiet eye that broods in sleep on his own heart." I have thought of you a *hundred* times, taking Nature by the hand and forcing from her the secrets (no difficult thing with a woman) she possesses. I am still very queer, one day well, one day ill.

Ere the close of his successful but weary life arrived, Watts Phillips was to enjoy one last gratifying theatrical triumph—the revival of his "Lost in London." He came from his sickroom to the theatre on the first night. "The piece was an immense success," he wrote, "the house crammed to suffocation, people standing on benches, and hundreds turned from the doors." He was ruffled, however, by a disagreeable incident.

"Emery has made his *mark*, and written me a noble letter. *Borrow the Times.* I had a row with Chatterton; I wouldn't come on after 2nd Act without Miss Foote, and I repudiated *then* as only being a revival after all; but I showed my pale mug—alas! alas! as you know—at the end. *Oh! if I had but health!* Poor Mrs. F. saw nothing, and all that was seen of her was her nose—the *cram* was *awful.* I am very glad you did not hear the language that passed between Chatterton and Old Watts. It nearly smashed Ord, Oxenford, etc. etc. Good strong talk. I'd have brought on little Lydia Foote, but 'I can't and won't come on *twice*, and I'll go on at the end of the piece; or go on yourself, and call yourself the author, I *don't* care.' But it was all right at the successful end, and I did not get away from 'behind' till past two."

"*Oh! if I had but health!*" That was the last despairing aspiration of the toiling dramatist. But it may be doubted if this alone would have secured the success he wished for. For it did seem that with these ceaseless drafts upon his powers, he had, as it is called, outwritten himself.

Not three months after the above letter, on the 3rd December, 1874, Watts Phillips' long illness terminated, and terminated fatally.

He is buried in Brompton Cemetery. The friends among the many present who paid their last tribute to the dead were the veteran George Cruikshank, Alfred Phillips (his brother), Benjamin Webster, George Augustus Sala, Mr. Milbank, Mr. Chatterton, Mr. Samuel Emery, Mr. Churchill, Mr. George Belmore, Dr. Daniel, Mr. W. Sawyer, Mr. J. V. Howard, and Mr. Moy Thomas. A few ladies of the stage were also present, including Miss Georgina Hodson, Miss Genevieve Ward, and Mrs. Alfred Mellon.

APPENDIX.

THE majority of the following letters having been written in the early part of Watts Phillips' life, and referring but very slightly to his artistic or literary career, it was decided to place them as an appendix, in order that the thread of the narrative, which leads the reader step by step—it might be said letter by letter—through the preceding pages, should not be broken.

The chief of the correspondence, descriptive of Paris and the journey thither, was written about the years 1845 to 1848, during which period, with brief intervals, the writer resided as an art student in that capital.

While taking lessons in oil-painting Mr. Phillips had as a fellow-student for a time the now great master of the Pre-Raphaelite school, Holman Hunt, to whom he refers in the first letter.

MY DEAR ANNIE,

I am too busy to write more than to ask you to write. Holman Hunt is waiting for me to go down to his place at Chelsea to meet some friends, and I have a block to finish first.

I enclose a few of the least warm criticisms upon Hunt and Millais. It is now generally allowed that they are among the very greatest painters England has ever produced.

Millais touches my heart more than any artist I have ever looked upon, and Hunt performs perfect miracles with his brush, literally painting sunlight.

What a glorious thing for these two young men to have defied the Royal Academy—compelled them, by the power of their genius, to give their pictures room; and by the same power excelled every picture placed by their side. Compared with these two Pre-Raphaelite brethren the R.A.'s have a most sorry R.A. (array) to offer.

Expecting news,   Yours,
                                                        WATTS.

II.

TO HIS MOTHER.

Generally speaking, the first thing that strikes you on entering France is the butt-end of a gendarme's musket in the pit of your stomach, as you make a dart from the boat, without pausing to deliver your passport—a pleasant refresher to your memory.

I was an eye-witness to a most painful scene of man-catching. A little man, of the most prim and sedate appearance, a walking embodiment of "Chesterfield's Letters," stepped briskly from the packet; a dozen yards, and the jackals were upon him. Shade of Hogarth! to have seen that man's face! What, him! Touch him! Could a look have annihilated, there would have been an end of the matter. As it was, he struggled manfully, and at last, by an unexpected display of vigour, burst from their grasp. Alas! to exchange a Charybdis for a Scylla; or, in other words, he jumped from the frying-pan into the fire, for, panting with rage, he rushed headlong into the arms of a thick-bearded, brawny vagabond advancing up the quay, who, shouting out the name of his hotel, without more ado tucked the little gentleman under his arm and bore him off in triumph.

The last I saw of my persecuted friend were the soles of his boots, like Mahomet's coffin hanging midway between heaven and earth, as he vanished round the corner. For my own part, I surrendered my arms—that is, my luggage —without useless resistance, and was conducted quietly to my quarters, the Hôtel de Richelieu.

III.

To his Sister.

Rouen.

Rouen is full of the remnants of an age gone by houses in the last stage of dissolution; unpaved, sombre-looking streets, and darkling Gothic churches, while the new stuccoed Parisian-looking buildings that are everywhere springing into existence appear by contrast like glaring coloured patches on a beggar's garment. The churches are its gems, the cathedral in particular—that mountain of carved stone, emblem of that once massive religion, now passing, if not in reality passed, away. There is something about these Gothic churches, these monuments of men's skill and patience, that produces a feeling of pleasing melancholy ; you may run up the lofty flight of steps laughing and talking gaily ; in the same mood you may traverse the dark passage and push open the small portal at the end ; but then comes a check—you are in the presence of the grandeur of a past age. You see around you " a petrified religion," as the poet has called it. Your very footfall seems an intrusion ; stone figures, frowning sternly or smiling meekly from their niches, rebuke you into silence. The old women (always old women) kneeling before the various shrines, with low humming chant telling their beads, or stealing with noiseless step along the dim cloisters, are strangely in character with the scene around—they look so ancient, coeval, as it were, with the cathedral.

Here and there candles glimmering before the figure of the Virgin—the pictures, and, last of all, the organ music, that sublimest of harmonies, richest of melodies, and the effect is complete.

I quite agree with the great American when he says, " I like the silent church before the service begins better than any sermon." This sublime edifice would elevate the spirit more than listening to the humming of some drowsy pulpit drone, half God's good Sabbath, while the worn-out clerk browbeats his desk below.

For my part I want no Bible text expounded. If the preacher would touch my heart, the words must flow freely from his own. Let him speak of God, not of miracles of an age defunct. Why, the very fact of my standing *here alive* is a greater miracle than he can read me ; as are the refreshing rains that beat against the window or hang in glistening pearl-drops from the trees : the healthful breeze that shakes them on to the thirsting grass beneath, and the feathered songsters that carol forth His praise.

Nature is God's book, whose language goes to all men's hearts. We live in an age of facts, not fiction, and need no historical legends to fashion our religion.

IV.

THE SAME.

Paris.

You must see Paris. Beautiful, gay Paris, which not to know argues yourself unknown. In my part I'm like that greyhound which somebody so touchingly mentions, that, in the pleasures of the chase, ran itself down to a terrier. I've almost worked myself to death ; I intend to see everything. This morning swaggering along the Boulevards; this night dancing (a dance peculiarly my own, and which has excited some envy in Paris) my legs off with mad students and pale, over-worked grisettes, little sickly flowers who take an hour's pleasure out of the night to drown the feeling of the day's privations and the coming morrow's misery, as an Englishwoman takes spirits; dances and other amusements being prohibited, especially on a Sunday, by a Christian and humane Legislature.

You have no doubt heard of the great Columbus, when the vision of his life was realised, and the forest-clad shores of the New World rose, a pleasing barrier to his ocean progress ? or of Balboa, when, speechless with a proud emotion, he stood on the borders of the, until then, unknown Pacific, the first man of the Old World who had gazed upon its wilderness of waters ? or—as I am in the humour for similes—of Cortes, when, like an eagle from the mountain summit, he looked downward upon his regal quarry, the golden, gorgeous Mexico, that lay, a glittering paradise, at his feet ?

Their joy was great, I do not doubt, but nothing—I can assure you, nothing to what I felt when, standing the other day in—blissful locality—the Place Vendôme, the words— they should have been written in gold—*London Porter*, met my delighted vision.

How long I stood, like a second Belshazzar, intent upon the writing on the wall, I know not. A rough " Prenez garde ! " first awakened me to passing events, and I found myself seated on the kerbstone, while a grinning carrier strode onward with his burthen.

Another time I should have cursed, but now I smiled

K

upon the man, and, rising gracefully, crossed the road and —entered the shop.

As Walter Scott observes, "More it needs not here to tell." Oh! Shakespeare and Milton, Barclay and Perkins, Bacon and Newton, Truman and Hanbury, yours are indeed immortal names! But my feelings are carrying me away.

This wandering life suits me too well. There must be gypsy blood in my veins, I am sure. Were I left to my own inclination, with a light heart I should trudge southward to "the land where citron-apples bloom, and oranges, like gold in leafy gloom," gladden the soil, and where I could live—

> "With God's own profound
>   High above me, and round me the mountains,
> And under, the sea,
>   And with one, my heart to bear witness
> What was, and shall be."

Never more returning back to—

> "A land where merit starves—obscure,
> And Wisdom says, "be anything but—poor.""

Yours,

WATTS.

V

THE SAME.

Paris.

Thanks for last letter. The winter here is of the severest kind. The Seine is frozen over, and the air full of fine frost-powder, that pierces the skin like needles. Commodore Frost is advancing in good earnest, and it behoves everyone in self-defence to follow bluff old Collingwood's advice, and baffle the enemy by keeping up a *brisk fire.*

Strange to relate, I believe the Morgue to be at present without a tenant, the cold is so severe. One man was seen last evening endeavouring to make his way through the ice with a pickaxe; but after working for nearly an hour, he marched off in a passion, saying "a man might as well live and be miserable, as die so d—— hard as all that."

Of the Morgue, in a previous letter, Mr. Phillips writes :—

I have just returned from the Morgue, the place where the bodies of those found drowned are exposed for three days, to find a claimant for the empty casket. It is a gloomy square building, a portion of which, separated from the remainder by an iron railing, is lighted from above. Behind this railing the bodies are exposed on inclined benches, a small stream of water flowing over them from a tap at the head of each; their clothes hang against the wall. The whole has the smell of a vault.

This horrible place is seldom without its tenant. Last month it boasted of seven at one time. Two now were stretched out upon the bench; one, a middle-sized, robust man, whose broad, expansive chest and muscular development gave promise of a long life, the suspicion being that his death was from other hands than his own.

The other body was a suicide; its story might be read at a glance: a common case—man's perfidy, woman's shame. There she lay, a model, or rather an emanation *from* the sculptor; so marble white her limbs, the long dark hair streaming dankly around the rigid face, which, despite the unnatural lock of the jaw and bruised forehead, was stamped with that curse when conjoined with poverty —that bitter curse of beauty.

A woman informed me of her history. As I said, it was an old one—old as modern civilisation. Her father had been sent for, and was expected to see his daughter, the first time for ten years (he had turned her from his door then), in this place.

K 2

Leaning against the railing, sick at heart, standing as I
was before a palpable embodiment of Hood's touching lyric,
I figured her pale face turned from the pitiless city, and bent
over the dark waters of the Seine, that courted (and water,
especially by night, has that strange fascination) the fatal
plunge ; then—the hesitation, but for a moment, ere the
despairing leap was taken to "Anywhere, anywhere out of
the world " ; when I was startled by the noisy conversation
of a party behind me, who were—pitying ?—no, indulging in
ribald jokes upon that poor sleeping girl. I could have spat
in the fellows' faces (their pardon—gentlemen's—for their
coats were of the best cloth and newest cut), who could find
no fitter place for their brutality.   Chilled to the marrow, I
left the place ; and, should I stop another year in Paris, this
will be the first and *last* time that, of my own accord, I
visit the Morgue.

Ever yours,

WATTS.

VI.

MY DEAR FATHER,

I have but time to write a few lines.   Paris, as I suppose
you are by now aware, is in a state of revolution.   Skir-
mishes long and bloody have taken place; every street is
barricaded, and while I write the whole body of the people,
National Guards and all, are upon the march to the Tuileries.
I could not get out of Paris if I wished, the railways having
stopped, and all the barriers being in possession of the
people; however, I run but slight danger.

Imagine a night here: the tocsin sounding, the people
shouting, the rolling of the drums, and, above all, the roar
of the artillery.   The hospitals are full of wounded, and by
this time the dead may be counted by hundreds.

Rouen has marched down, likewise the people of Lyons.
We shall have desperate work if concessions of rights, long

promised, long deferred, are not made to an indignant people. If it be possible, can you forward me any money ? *I* do not know whether the post will run. Can you send me thirty pounds ? The. bakers' shops (as every other) are closed, and it is a favour to get provisions. Prices have, of course, gone up incredibly. This cannot last long. Two or three days must settle it, without the troops still hold out.

Three o'clock.

The king has abdicated. A National Assembly is declared. Glorious things are expected. Liberty *has* dawned on France. Hurrah ! More anon. Of course agitation still continues, etc.

VII.

The Same.

Boulogne-sur-Mer.

Lord Normanby (British Ambassador) having advised me to leave Paris, I arrived here this morning, and have taken up my habitation in my old quarters. The town is full of English who have left Paris, and are *en route* for England, some being in such haste as to have left by fishing-boats ; all of which fear is very much exaggerated ; the only *real* danger being in Paris, where indeed it exists to strangers in no small degree, and will continue to do so until the fierce mob, the very refuse of the galleys and scum of the capital, is disarmed and sent to the frontiers. They have already completely sacked the Tuileries, and burnt a portion of the Palais Royal.

Many châteaux on the outskirts have been plundered and their grounds devastated. The royal residence of Neuilly has been burnt; numbers who had found their way to the cellars perishing at the same time. They have threatened to destroy the principal residences in Paris; but the National Guard are under arms night and day, while the soldiers of the line are getting back *their* arms, so we may soon hope to see quiet and safety once more restored.

VIII.

His Sister.

Paris.

Back once again in Paris. I wish you could come over, as anything in the shape of description must fall short of the original. In old Paris I revel—what with the Luxembourg at the other side of the great city, the Jardin des Plantes—the most splendid botanical collection in the world—the Louvre and Versailles, to which all Paris is but a gew-gaw, to whose majestic splendour no pen can do justice. And what more can tourists look for ? Unless it be Père-la-Chaise, the cemetery, which acts as a sedative to a fever of enjoyment—the City of Hope, as this place has been called.

> " All earth is but an hour-glass, and the sands
>   That tremble through, are *men* /"

When wandering, as I like to do, through this romantic yet tomb-like garden, reading the many inscriptions—so varied in their expression, yet all embodying the same thing—Hope—the lines of the great German poet seem strikingly apt—

> " When we sink in the grave, why the grave has scope,
>   And over the coffin man planted—hope.
>   And it is not a dream of a fancy proud,
>   With a fool for its dull begetter ;
>   There's a voice at the heart proclaims *aloud*,
>   " We're born for a something better ! "
>   And that voice of the heart, oh ! ye may believe
>   Will never the hope of the soul deceive."

The women of Paris are, after all, the most attractive part of it. They might be studied with some advantage by their sisters in England. There is no woman in the world who can invest the driest of topics, or most trivial of subjects, with such interest and charm as she does by the grace, vivacity of her delivery. And then her dress—no matter whether costly silk or humble cotton, it is fashioned with a tasteful elegance rarely seen elsewhere ; the jaunty cap, the set of the shawl, the very cock of the bonnet—if I may use such a Gothic expression—sets rivalry at defiance. It's an art scarcely to be obtained, and when obtained cannot be valued too highly.

Besides, what woman understands the "poetry of motion" like a French lady or French grisette ? It's born with them. An English child may be said "to go alone," to toddle ; an English woman to march, to progress, to step out; but the French woman *walks.*

Now, in personal beauty our countrywomen bear away the palm, but it is, nine cases out of ten, beauty without expression. This is the reason why plain girls in England are always the most interesting, amiable, and agreeable. They place their dependence upon the solid qualities of pleasing, and are composed of "such stuff as *good* wives are made of," while their handsome rivals find too late that men soon tire of a show of lifeless waxwork.

I have met with many a girl, quite destitute of personal beauty of countenance, who, during the evening, has so redeemed the want by her lively manner and vivacious conversation that her chair has been the centre of attraction, while many a fair-cheeked doll has sat silent in a corner.

IX.

HIS FATHER.

Paris.

Now for a bit of the world I live in. France is at present in that turbulent state that you quiet inhabitants of the United Queendoms can scarcely form a conception. Every man in the shape of anything like self-esteem is putting up as President for this unfortunate Republic, for which onerous office most of the candidates are about as fitted as George I. was to become King of England, and *his* chief qualification was, I believe, that he could speak no English. The election of Louis Napoleon is certain.

The Rouge Republicans are busy here plotting and scheming. According to their doctrines, the only true method for a liberation is that France, like the Israelites of old, should first pass through a Red Sea.

They overlook the many bright names in the stormy history of France's past, to grasp at those of Robespierre, St. Just, Marat, and Danton, those mighty monsters, begotten, like those of the Nile, from corruption. They neglect or scoff at the milder and better lights, chaining themselves to no creed, no belief but that propounded by these "men without a God."

At the present moment it is only the strictest vigilance— the soldiers in the barrack and public buildings—the *hourly* patrol—that keep Paris from revolt.

Poor Paris ! Like the fable of the Pelican, it seems her fate to feed her numerous progeny with her blood. Each and all are politicians now—restless poverty has found a voice, and plots in secret. Every quack has his antidote for social evils, knowing as much what are and ought to be constitutions and liberties as the elder Weller when he speaks about " that gallant old Carter who stood up for our liberties, and won 'em too."

I came home last evening over the Pont Neuf, and stopped for some minutes to look at the crowd of buildings (the Cité) which formed the gloomy masses that stretched along the river's banks—the faint and flickering lights that shone on the dark waters—the tall towers of the various edifices, all so quiet and yet so grand in their indistinctness—when I was roughly disturbed in my meditations by crowds of fellows marching (from some banquet, I imagine) over the bridge, and roaring the revolutionary songs. No sooner were they passed than a body of the Garde Mobile succeeded, their bayonets glistening in the moonlight.

The *Ça ira* still ringing in my ears, I walked on, musing upon the scene, which might have been an extract from the great drama of the First Republic; and when I looked up —standing in the old Place de la Révolution—I almost expected to see the tall, gaunt form of the guillotine, show-ing black against the sky, and blasting, like the upas, with its hideous aspect the passers by.

I am glad to find the information concerning the death of Macready was unfounded, though by all accounts he still remains a stiff-'un. (Oh—oh—run for the police!)

Is it true that "The Bohemian Girl" has again become popular? How I detest Balfe, whose jingles are only worthy to be allied with the effusions of the poet Bunn. He can only be popular with the uncultivated millions. To those who recognise music as the "poetry of sound," such a man must be an abhorrence. Popularity is no proof of merit; but alas! for taste in England, when the composi-tions of such men as Mozart, Weber, Beethoven—great Beethoven, wildest, grandest, most poetical of composers— Meyerbeer, and a host of others, immortal men who *cannot* die, are superseded by the twitterings of "The Bohemian Girl" and others of her class.

We talk of the march of intellect! What would our forefathers have said, to know their old madrigals, songs, and lyrics—those bits of melodies of which the words themselves are music—are shelved, giving place to the rhapsodies of a Fitzball and the tunes of hurdy-gurdy Balfe?

I must stop here. Don't be alarmed at any rumour you hear in England, where a "bombast" becomes a war, and a street row a revolution. Though there may be great *fear*, there is but little *danger*.

X.

To Mr. F. Jones.

Jeudi.

The letter of M. le Barren Jones has but this moment arrived (10 o'clock). His Excellency and Serene Holiness Cardinal Phillips has in half an hour from the present time to take part in a funeral ceremony: attending at the church, and afterwards to the cemetery, one of his friends in Paris.

Nothing dispels a *black* cloud so quickly as sunshine, and the arrival of the Barren Jones will be a bright ray in the present gloom that surrounds His Excellency..

M. le Cardinal Phillips will be at M. le Barren's hotel at 2 o'clock, if not before, unless he hears from that distinguished personage to the contrary.

When the funeral is over, his black garments will disappear for the more gorgeous plumage of the peacock, and a smile will replace the tear—sich is life.

XI.

To Miss Phillips.

Honor Oak Villas,
Forest Hill,
27.10.52.

I hasten to make you partakers in a bit of good news.

I was dining with a party of friends at their club (the Reform), when, Thackeray being in the room, our conversation turned on *Punch*. Philp said that he had often thought of attempting a periodical of a similar nature, always thinking that capital would buy talent; but—"they were at a loss for a good name." I at once proposed

"*Diogenes,*" the observer of manners and cynic philosopher It was received with much applause. After that we adjourned, and the matter was dropped. We have dined several times at the club since, but the conversation has never been renewed.

On Saturday, to my surprise, Philip came down to Forest Hill, stated that all arrangements were made, and proposed that I should assist him in conducting the journal. I agreed. An agreement has been signed for six months at six pounds a week ; at the end of that time, should the paper succeed, to be *considerably increased.*

Yours, etc.,

WATTS.

XII.

To E. W. PHILLIPS.

11, *Hills Place,*
Oxford Street.

I am sure you will pardon my not having replied before to your question whether I am able to furnish a story or stories to a new magazine. The fact is, I was unwilling to say "No" as long as there was a possibility of my doing so ; but, as I feared, my time just now is so occupied that I can only think of my stage engagements, which are so pressing that I have had to withdraw from my offer of a series of articles for the *Daily News,* made to my friend Mr. Labouchere. I have a new piece commissioned, also a comedy. Under these circumstances I am "fettered" [the title of one of his dramas] for a few months. Etc.

XIII.

A FRAGMENT.

After "Lost in London," I believe in the evil eye Neville was saying to me a few days ago that he thought every actor and actress in London must in course of time have a "turn" at "Lost in London," and has just illustrated his own jest. Playing with a loaded revolver, he has sent a small bullet through his hand—a very nasty wound—and *Phillips* acted the part last night. I went with Knight and Tomlins to the Arundel yesterday evening; this final change was welcomed with roars of laughter. I recommended the head-carpenter last night to understudy Job, in case Phillips, etc. etc. He promised he would.

XIV.

MY DEAR DOCTOR [CANTON],

Webster (and Webster only) is coming to my place *at half-past five sharp* to-morrow for a *chat* and a slice (nothing more) of Dartmoor mutton. Mind, that's all; but then there's the chat, which you can so greatly assist in. Will you come *en famille* and *sans cérémonie?* If so, send a telegram that I may order an extra potato. Please say " Yes" or "No." Say "Yes."

I make no apology for this brief invitation, but W—— only said, "I'll come and have a gossip to-morrow," and I know we shall be cosy with *you.*

Sincerely and affectionately yours,

WATTS PHILLIPS.

XV.

TO E. W. PHILLIPS.

The Firs, Edenbridge.

I know *nothing* about "Marlborough," nor "Yvonne," nor "Amos." Absolutely nothing. Vining came down here for me to read the piece to him. His conception of Marlborough is *admirable.* His notion of the part is wonderfully good. He thinks, and Canton says that Webster told him, Canton, last week, Marlborough and the Duchess are two of the finest *rôles* in the modern drama.

My dear old friend Dr. Canton came down last Saturday, staying till Monday. He brought me a very pretty present in the shape of a breast-pin, consisting of a solid gold nugget.

Yours affectionately,

WATTS.

XVI.

THE SAME.

The Firs, Edenbridge.

Nothing new about " Amos." The Rousbys yet rule the roast. " Marlborough " is still with his legs in the stocks, much to my annoyance, for Edwin Booth has offered to purchase the right to play it in America—a great actor. Webster refuses even to answer Vining's letter, and the latter is now savage against everybody, and can't move one way or the other.

Capital letter, and capital fellow, Labouchere. A good friend to me. Poor Paris indeed! I can't write about it. Coleridge was right when he compared the French nation to a barrel of gunpowder. Half the Communists were honest, single-minded, pure-hearted men ; the other half infernal scoundrels who would have burnt their own mothers for a franc and a half a day.

I am contemplating a drama with the Franco-Prussian War for a background. I don't think the idea a bad one.

The two dramas mentioned in the *Athenæum* and elsewhere are our old friends "Amos" and " Yvonne's Revenge." Owing to the continued talk about "Amos," by some means

the *book* [the novel written by Mr. Phillips some years pre-
viously] has got over to America, and is announced, with
" Canary Bird," to appear as the *"feuilletons"* in a leading
New York paper, by " Fairfax Balfour " ! ! !

Leicester Wallack, who has got copies of the drama in
readiness to bring out simultaneously with its production
here, sends me the enclosed extracts, adding, " I fear it will
lose you your chance over here, for it is *certain* to be
dramatised. I thought the stories (' Amos ' and ' Canary
Bird ') were out of print ? It is a serious loss to you, this
procrastination in England."

How *could* " Amos " have got to America just at this
present time ? I *know* neither of the stories can be pro-
cured at the publisher's, who says they are out of print. It
puzzles me, and looks like malice. Isn't all this like my
luck ?

Tell J. J—— I congratulate him on his success.

Yours, etc.

WATTS.

THE END.

PRINTED BY CASSELL & COMPANY, LIMITED, LA BELLE SAUVAGE, LONDON, E.C.